It is called Pitfall, at the Dragon's Claw.

He travels the galaxy to find it, and once he does, he is determined to face off against any others who want to win.

His name is Mike Murray, and he wants to be the best racer this solar system—or any other—has ever known.

His future awaits him at Clypsis.

Bantam Spectra Books
Ask your bookseller for the titles you have missed

ROGER ZELAZNY'S

ALIEN SPEEDWAY

BOOK **1**: CLYPSIS

ROGER ZELAZNY'S

ALIEN SPEEDWAY

BOOK 1: CLYPSIS

by Jeffrey A. Carver

A BYRON PREISS BOOK

BANTAM BOOKS

TORONTO • NEW YORK • LONDON • SYDNEY • AUCKLAND

ROGER ZELAZNY'S ALIEN SPEEDWAY
BOOK 1: CLYPSIS
A Bantam Spectra Book / October 1987

*The author gratefully acknowledges the songwriting
of Crystal Nash and of Destiny Quibbler whose work
provided the inspiration for the songs portrayed in this book.*

*Special thanks to Lou Aronica, Amy Stout, Kirby McCanley,
Joan Brandt, and Steve C. Ringgenberg.*
Cover art by Bob Eggleton.
Cover design by Alex Jay.
Interior illustrations by Hayashi.
All rights reserved.

Bantam Books are published by Bantam Books, Inc. Its trademark, consisting of the words ''Bantam Books'' and the por-
trayal of a rooster, is Registered in U.S. Patent and Trademark
Office and in other countries. Marca Registrada. Bantam
Books, Inc., 666 Fifth Avenue, New York, New York 10103.

This story is dedicated to several friends who, by the most remarkable of coincidences, might resemble certain characters portrayed within. You know who you are.

INTRODUCTION

Long before I wrote *Damnation Alley* I knew a certain fascination for fast, powerful vehicles. I do not know whether this had anything to do with having grown up on a street where drag racers could regularly be heard revving their engines late at night, followed by the shriek of tires as they took off, generally in the direction of Lakeland Boulevard. Occasionally, there would be an accident, and once a fellow I knew made the front page of the local paper by emerging unscathed from a totalled vehicle, just a few doors up the street from me.

And it was only five years ago that I took up skiing, almost by chance. I discovered that I liked the slick slopes and the feel of the wind, though I doubt I will ever be a great skier and I have no desire to race with anyone. But there is something I find very pleasing to the rapid cutting of my own geodesic with only the bare elements for company. For me, it is a pleasant way of getting rid of myself occasionally, as thinking ceases and I merely respond to the mountainside.

In this context I recall, too, that one of my early reading pleasures was the writings of Saint-Exupery, in his poetic descriptions of the youthful days of air flight when the pilot was almost one with his craft.

Now, it has often struck me that there is nearly always a good story to be had in dealing with extremes—the biggest or the smallest of something, the first, the last. So when a notion involving the biggest racetrack and the fastest vehicles came up, I pursued it.

The Alien Speedway series was, in effect, to be the story of the Big Racetrack in the Sky, the place where the greatest racers and the fastest vehicles would come together for the most exciting races ever run. It was also to be the story of a young man whose great desire was to go there and become a part of it, to race. . . .

I developed the general concept and background for the series and provided some narrative outlines, guides and ideas. I gave it considerable thought and, strangely, I put most of it to paper at the Santa Fe ski basin, over endless cups of hot chocolate and many donuts, occasionally looking up to watch the glissandos of dark or brightly clad people descending the slopes. It was a fine place to work on something like this, because of the mood as well as the view. People were constantly coming and going, talking about the condition of the slopes, about accidents, about equipment. Very strangely, at one point, Richard Sealey came in from skiing and stopped to ask me what the hell I was doing scribbling away there. Now, he is the author of an automotive column for a major Sunday supplement, has written books on the VW Rabbit and the Subaru, and he used to race professionally himself, as well as being an experienced pit-man. I told him a bit about the idea, which he found intriguing, and he kindly offered me the loan of a number of interesting-sounding books on auto racing. The need for them did not really arise, as it turned out, but I tend to take any kind of synchronicity on the eve of a project as something of a good omen. The mood continued and I kept writing. I did not finish the work that day, but returned to the same place later to complete it, solely because the atmosphere there seemed extremely right for it.

The greatest racetrack, I decided, would be an entire solar system engineered to provide the courses. The vehicles would be hot little fusion-powered ships, constantly accelerating and decelerating. I was picturing massive, lengthy, Indianapolis Five Hundred-type events in different parts of the system. It was put to me, though, that faster races over much greater distances would be even more desirable in terms of flashy imagery, added danger and the number of events to be run. It then became a collaborative effort on this and other matters, with the authors who would actually be doing the hands-on work with this universe I had been putting together. The good old alien artifact trick could be invoked for the initial teleportation-like space shortcuts for startups, and for the setting up of extra-universal race lanes for superluminal effects. The bugs in the Clypsis system were swatted or sprayed, and the desired picture of the Big Track, of Pitfall at the Dragon's Claw, of the entire milieu, emerged, the appropriate backdrop for the story of Mike Murray, the kid who would race.

I read the stories as they were created, and I was fascinated to see what the authors did with the material. It is like listening to jazz variations on a familiar theme to see hot new writers take a set of premises and play off of them. A little further along the way I saw some of the artwork—very appropriate—by Hayashi, and was pleased at the irony of his being a designer for Honda. Everything concerned with the project was falling into smooth synch, for which I was grateful.

A word or two might be in order here on the notion of the "recorded" character of Speedball Raybo and those of his like who, while physically dead, continue to exist in a peculiar electronic fashion. The technology of this period permits a much more elaborate brain scan than that of a simple electroencephalograph. Devices of sufficient sophistication have been developed to permit the monitoring of the total pattern of the brain's activity. When conducted at appropriate length and depth these scans can assess and encode the complex workings of the psyche to the extent where an actual record of the individual is created—an almost complete image of the character and personality of a person, along with the collection of memories, tastes, habits and talents possessed at the time the record is made. This procedure is valuable for a number of reasons. In the event of an accident resulting in brain damage, the medical technology exists to stimulate the DNA to promote regeneration of the damaged neural tissue. Skills or memories localized in these areas, lost through the trauma and absent from the pattern of the new tissue, may be supplied from the personal record of the individual on file in the Brain Bank and imprinted from this upon the new cells. Recent memories or very new skills, of course, are not present in this record, as it only contains those materials which were present at the time the recording was made. This is why the people undergo periodic updating of their neurological records.

While the procedure first began as a medical-therapeutic adjunct, it was later realized that a recorded personality could be activated within the Brain Bank for purposes of obtaining a unique perspective on events—even after the death of the recorded individual. The next step involved the development of a means for recalling such an individual as a physically functioning entity by imprinting the recorded psyche on an electromechanical brain contained within a robot body. Such individuals may be peculiarly valuable as teachers, researchers, investigators. Hence, the late Speedball Raybo may be found occupying an artificial body, functioning as a living entity. He remembers everything about himself except for his own death and the weeks preceding it, as these were subsequent to his final recording session.

Not everybody, of course, is as tough-minded as Speedball. While pilots and racing officials have their psyches recorded for medical or informational purposes, not all of them are necessarily candidates for recall in robot bodies. Great batteries of psychological tests are administered to those who are recorded, resulting in an assessment as to whether one could adjust to existence in such a revised form. For some, the notion strikes at the very roots of identity, and anxiety or dangerous phobias would be manifest in the event of a re-animation. The existence of a robot gone psycho is not desirable; therefore, many individuals would not undergo this incarnation of awareness, and only the information from their minds would be preserved, sans awareness.

There are also procedures for a living individual's interfacing with the Brain Bank data-net, in whole or in part, for various research purposes—or for an individual suffering from major injuries to have his/her consciousness transferred to it for purposes of pursuing daily affairs remotely while the body remains under medical treatment. And even an artificial construction of the Brain Bank might be embodied. For that matter, one could also possibly encounter an earlier recorded version of oneself moving about in a mechanical body, though there are regulations against such doppelgangering except under unusual circumstances.

All of this serves to make life at Pitfall an unusual mixture of individuals.

Any sort of collaborative effort is bound to be a bit tricky. I learned this in writing stories myself set in universes created by others, such as those of Larry Niven and Fred Saberhagen, and in participating in the creation of shared-world books, such as the Wild Card series edited by George R. R. Martin. In some respects the process is easier than going it on your own, because a lot of the background material is already in place. In other ways it is more difficult, in that the nature of the setup includes constraints one might not ordinarily place upon oneself, with the necessary facing of problems one might feel inclined to write around. I suppose that the simplest way of putting it, having seen the process from both sides, is that it is different yet familiar, an interesting and instructive experience. I am fascinated and pleased by the work which has been done on this project—and entertained as well, which is one of the main reasons I'm in this game.

So, the track is ready and the atoms are fusing. There's the start signal. The way is clear.

HIT IT.

—Roger Zelazny
Santa Fe, 1987

CHAPTER 1

The music cut off from Mike Murray's ears as he left the shuttle tube. He kept singing as he strode down the walkway toward his aunt's house: "Hit me on the upside . . . and I'll bring you to the downside. . . ." As he hit a sharply rising note, he heard a familiar crackling sound. He looked up to see a power beam lancing across the sky, and at its tip a freighter blazing free of Earth and leaping toward space.

He ran to follow its progress, ducking to get a view between buildings until the ship finally vanished, high in the eastern sky. It wouldn't yet have acquired orbital velocity, but in a few moments it would pick up another power beam from a station a hundred kilometers off the Florida coast, which would give it a final kick toward orbit.

One of these days, Mike thought with a sigh. Of course, it wasn't freighters, but fusion racers, that were the stuff of his dreams. That was how he planned to go into space one day. But for now, it was just a dream. He had school to finish, and two years before his legal independence, and . . . Ah, why think about it, anyway? With a wistful sigh, he fished in his pocket for a Georgia macanut and nibbled at its sweet, glazed surface as he continued on his way home.

He was still a block and a half from home when he rounded the corner at the end of the street—and realized that something was wrong. There was a bleep-ball outside

1

his aunt's front door—a floating ball of blue lightning, bright even in the afternoon sun. Cops—what were they doing at his aunt's house? He stopped and scowled. It couldn't be something he'd done, could it? No, he hadn't *done* anything—at least not recently.

A cold premonition touched him in the pit of his stomach. His feet began moving in a run before his brain had a chance to catch up. He covered the distance in half a minute, but that was long enough for a policeman to walk out of the house and disappear into the bleep-ball. "Hey!" Mike shouted—but he was already gone. The sparkling ball of light remained; there had to be more cops inside.

Sprinting to the door, he nearly collided with a policeman coming out. "Watch it there, sonny!" the officer barked.

Mike caught his breath and backed away. The cop was heavyset, with dark, bushy eyebrows, and he had a powerful odor of garlic and onions on his breath. Mike gagged. "I'm . . . What's happening in there?"

"Is that any of your business? What do you want to know for?" the cop asked suspiciously.

"I live here! Where's my aunt?"

"Your aunt?" The policeman grunted. "You mean the lady who lives here? Mrs. Quaid? They took her out about fifteen minutes ago."

"*What?* Took her where?"

"The hospital, I think. Ask Officer Newman, inside—" The cop grabbed at Mike as he began to push past. "Hey—I'm not done talking—"

Mike wrenched his arm loose and darted into the house. He heard the cop shouting after him, but he was too furious to care. In the den he found an officer standing at the home-control computer, typing something in.

The officer looked up as Mike asked, "Are you—"

"Officer Newman. You the young man who lives here? Mike—"

"Yeah. Murray. Mike Murray. What's this about my Aunt Anna? What's happened to her?"

"Mrs. Quaid was rushed to the emergency ward just

a few minutes ago. Some sort of allergy attack, apparently. She was having trouble breathing.''

"Allergy attack?" Mike was puzzled. "But she's not allergic to anything . . ."

The cop nodded. "You'll have to come down to the station with—"

"Is she all right?"

"We haven't heard yet. As soon as we get a statement from you, we'll take you down to find out."

Mike was stunned. In the four years he'd lived with her, his aunt had never been sick, not even for a day. How could she suddenly—

"We're finished here, so if you'll just come with me," Officer Newman was saying.

"Take me to see her first! I have a right to know if she's all right!"

The cop gazed at him curiously. "Pretty close to your aunt, are you?"

Now, what kind of a question was that?

"I ask because I just checked your record, and I see you've been in trouble more than once in the last few years." Officer Newman's tone wasn't exactly accusing, but came close. "I found truancy, after-hours trespassing at the spaceport . . ."

"Look—I was just trying to go for some simulator time, and I—" Mike found himself without words. Why was he suddenly having to defend himself?

Officer Newman nodded, not unkindly. "You don't have to explain it to me. But since you're underage, and for the moment without an able guardian, you'll have to come to the station first. We'll make out a report, and then we'll get you to see your aunt."

Mike choked down a protest.

"Let's go," said the officer, pointing the way out.

As if he didn't know the way out of his own home. Mike glanced around the den with a shiver, as though it would never be the same again. Don't be morbid, he thought. Tomorrow everything will be back to normal.

As they stepped outside, the officer waved his partner

on. The first cop disappeared into the bleep-ball with a flash of blue light. Officer Newman gestured to Mike to follow. He hesitated; only once had he ever been through one of these things, when he'd been picked up in the middle of the night at the spaceport. It gave him a funny feeling to remember that now.

The policeman nudged him. He took a breath and walked forward. The world went blank with a blue-white flash, and he felt a tingle over every inch of his body as he blinked and stepped out into the crowded lobby of the precinct station.

"Mike MacAlister Murray . . . uh-huh . . . Place of birth?" the clerk's voice droned.

"Cleveland."

"Uh-huh . . . It says here your folks are deceased . . ."

"Right."

"Tube accident, four years ago?"

"Right."

". . . and one Anna Quaid is your legal guardian . . ."

"Yes."

"Uh-huh . . . you're sixteen . . . Where's your closest living relative?"

Pause. "Don't have any . . ."

It took nearly an hour, but eventually they'd picked him clean of information—they'd had it all, anyway, but had insisted on his repeating everything for the record—and finally Officer Newman took him to another ball of lightning. Mike walked into it.

He stepped out into the lobby of the St. Jameson's Emergency Medical Room. With a quick look around to get his bearings, he hurried to the information desk, with Officer Newman right behind him. He tried not to be self-conscious of the highly visible manner of his arrival. "Mrs. Anna Quaid," he said to the automaton on duty.

"What about her?" asked the automaton.

Stupid machine! "She was brought in . . ."

"As a patient?" the machine asked politely.

"Yes—she—"

4

"Was brought in as a code-three emergency, precinct five," Officer Newman snapped.

"One moment, please."

Mike waited impatiently for the automaton to provide more information; he was so intent on it that he failed to see the white-uniformed woman approaching. He looked up when he heard Officer Newman say, "This is Mrs. Quaid's nephew."

The woman, short with light curly hair, nodded. Mike swallowed. "Is she—all right?" he said with difficulty.

"I'll have to check," she said quietly. "My name is Ms. May. I've been assigned as your advocate-adviser. If you'll wait a moment, please."

Advocate-adviser? They'd assigned one of those when his parents had died. Mike started to ask, then thought better of it.

Ms. May spoke quickly to the automaton. She frowned and bent to look at a display screen. After a moment, she straightened, a sober expression on her face. "You're the ward of Mrs. Quaid?" Mike nodded, and her frown deepened. "I'm sorry," she said at last. "Your aunt has died in emergency care."

Mike's breath escaped in disbelief. "What?" he whispered. *"How?"*

"She was brought in unconscious, not breathing— apparently in a severe reaction to a beajangle sting."

"What?" He scarcely spoke the question aloud.

"You know what a beajangle is?"

Mike nodded, stunned. Of course he knew. It was a damned alien insect that was infesting half the Southern Hemisphere—all because of some careless shippers who'd allowed their larvae to get aboard freighters traveling from Gliese 95 to Sol. But they weren't this far north! "That can't be!" he croaked.

"I'm afraid there have already been several cases in Florida this year," Ms. May said.

"But—people don't die of it! You can treat it! *Can't you?*"

Her expression darkened. "There are people with

unusual sensitivities. Unfortunately, it seems there was confusion about the diagnosis, and your aunt was initially given the wrong antitoxin. By the time the mistake was discovered . . .'' She scowled. ''It was too late. She died forty minutes ago.''

Mike choked with disbelief. His eyes stung; they were growing damp. ''How . . . how can that be?''

''Well—it's my job to help you find out. We'll have to—*Wait, please!*''

Mike staggered back from her. He was suffocating; he needed air. It was a bad dream, surely. Not his aunt . . . she *couldn't* have died . . . he had no one left, if she was gone . . . *how could they have killed her?*

''Hey, there, son. Get a grip. I know it's tough.'' Officer Newman had a tight lock on his arm.

Mike shivered and nodded numbly. There would be hearings now, and questions. The foster agency . . .

''You okay?'' asked the cop. ''You want to sit down?''

Mike nodded. With Ms. May leading the way, he walked with the officer to a small alcove off the lounge. They sat quietly a few moments, and then Ms. May and Officer Newman began to discuss what would happen next. Ms. May asked Mike if his aunt had been brain-taped in case of accidental death.

Mike shook his head. ''She's not . . . she wasn't rich. Look—I need to go to the can for a minute. All right?''

The officer studied him for a moment before nodding, and Ms. May pointed, and he took a deep breath and strode across the lobby. He opened the door to the men's room and went in and leaned over the sink, trembling . . . staring at his reflection in the mirror . . . running his hands through his thatch of dark hair. Thinking.

What now? He'd been through this before, after his parents' deaths. He knew the drill. First he'd have to go back with the cop. The police would dump him into an agency full of social workers and bureaucrats, and he'd probably never sleep in his own bed again. Devil only knew where he'd wind up this time.

Screw that, he thought. He blinked rapidly; his reflection was blurring. He ran some cold water from the tap and stared at it absently before finally bending down to splash his face. He straightened up, gasping from the cold.

For the second time in his life, his world had been turned upside down. After his parents' deaths, he'd been in one foster home after another, until his aunt finally had sent for him in Florida. Maybe she'd never really understood him; still, she'd tried, she'd treated him well. But he'd just never felt right here, never at home. Except for the spaceport nearby . . . but then, that was just dreams, wasn't it?

Wasn't it?

He dried his face.

It was hard to believe how coolly he was reacting to this. His aunt was gone. He couldn't do anything for her now. He had only himself to think of. And that meant one thing. Getting out.

Act at once—or lose the chance, he knew.

"All right," he murmured. He walked to the door and opened it cautiously, peering in the direction of the alcove on the other side of the lounge. Several large palms partially obstructed the view; he couldn't quite see whether Officer Newman or Ms. May were watching for him. He took a silent breath—and slipped down the corridor in the other direction.

Expecting to hear the policeman's voice at any moment, heart pounding, he walked quickly through a set of double doors, turned right down a tiled hallway, hurried past rows of people waiting on clinic benches, and almost broke into a run when he saw an exit sign at the end of the corridor. He forced himself to walk. He passed under the exit sign, hurried down some steps, and pushed open a door.

The sun caught him full in the face. He sighed with relief, leaning for a moment against the outer wall. Was he ready for this? As of this moment, he was a fugitive. But he was free.

He swallowed, then set out down the street at a run, turning at the first corner. He never looked back.

*   *   *

Officer Newman nodded, not really listening to whatever Ms. May was saying. He hated this part of the job, dealing with family tragedies, especially when there was really nothing that could be done for the people. Take this Murray kid: he'd be dumped back into the foster-care system and probably bounced around until he turned eighteen. Not that there weren't good foster families around—but it was tough to place a sixteen-year-old kid who'd had even a minor brush or two with the law. And what kind of life was that for a kid?

He was keeping an eye out where the kid had disappeared, glancing back and forth between Ms. May and the men's-room door. Ms. May was dictating a preliminary report on the case into a small cube, and at her request, Officer Newman leaned toward the cube and briefly summarized the circumstances under which Mrs. Quaid had been found by the police after a bio-alert warning was received at the station, and all the rest—there was no end to the red tape in this job, and that was another thing he hated. What was taking the kid so long, anyway?

He craned his neck past a couple of palms that were blocking his view. No one was going in or out of the men's room. "Excuse me," he said to Ms. May, rising abruptly. Ignoring her startled look, he walked across the lobby, pursing his lips. It took him no more than thirty seconds to determine that there was no one at all in the men's room, and the Murray kid was nowhere else in sight; he'd flown the coop.

Cursing silently, he pressed a button on his left collar. "This is Newman," he muttered. "I'm at St. Jameson's. I need a locate-and-detain on one Michael MacAlister Murray, sixteen years, five eight, one-fifty-five pounds, dark hair..."

Mike spent the rest of the day hiding in the hedges of his neighbor's back yard. Old Man Poswolsky had a regular jungle of bushes back there, but he didn't go outside much anymore, because of his arthritis, so it was probably a safe bet to huddle back here—out of the range

8

of the surveillance module the cops had left on Aunt Anna's house. What he was hoping was that he could figure out a way to get back into the house without setting off any alarms and bringing the police back down on him. It was a faint hope, at best; but all of his belongings, except the clothes on his back, were in that house.

He'd risked one call, from a pay booth, before coming here; he'd called one of his friends who worked out at the spaceport and pleaded for a favor—a big one. Kenny had promised to try, but what Mike was asking, Kenny couldn't do alone. If he could enlist the aid of a few other guys on the docks, then maybe there was a chance. He'd told Mike to come to the spaceport a little before midnight, when his shift came on, and they'd see. It wasn't a great chance, but it was the only one Mike had.

Huddling under a bush as the evening slowly wore on, Mike had plenty of time to think about the unfairness of it all—too much time, maybe. Second thoughts weren't all that helpful when you were about to do something that your gut said was right but your brain and everything you'd ever been taught said was wrong. He reminded himself of the alternatives, and swallowed hard, and tried to think instead about the possibilities if he succeeded. And he shivered continually, because it got awfully cold and lonely sitting on the ground long after dark.

The surveillance monitor glimmered in reflected street-light as it orbited above his aunt's house, a thin slip of silver. It never ceased its patrol; its attention never wavered.

Mike watched it as the hours crawled by, realizing slowly that in this, at least, he was defeated. He was *not* going to be able to slip past the monitor; it was too good, too diligent. That meant he'd be leaving behind his computer storage chips containing his books and his piloting manuals, his clothes, and food and money, and anything else he might have recovered. He shivered, blowing into his hands. He shivered from the cold, but from fear and loneliness, too. Reaching into his jacket pocket, he found one last maca-nut. He turned it over in his hand for a few seconds, then chewed it slowly, savoring the taste. Reluctantly, and a little angrily, he made his decision and rose.

It was time to leave.

It was close to midnight by the time Mike stole across the freight receiving area at the edge of the Canaveral Spaceport, avoiding the main entrance. Against the dark eastern sky, the launcher-derricks and waiting ships were illuminated by scattered arrays of floodlights. It took him only a few minutes to reach the loading-dock area where he'd worked as a part-time helper last summer. He slipped into the number-two hangar by the side door, and after peering around silently, made his way past the dark, massive shape of a freighter, toward the rear of the hangar where he and his work buddies used to loaf when there was nothing urgent to be done. The place was gloomy and quiet at this hour, but that would change after the loading shift came on.

"Hello?" he heard, from the far side of the hangar. "Who's there?"

Mike tensed for an instant, then relaxed. "Me," he said. "Mike." He walked into the light on the far side of the freighter and saw a tall, lanky figure walking toward him. "Hi, Kenny."

"You're early," Kenny said.

"Yeah." Mike tipped his head back and gazed up at the silent space freighter. For a moment he just stared, imagining that finely pitted hull hurtling across the sky toward the orbiting docks, and he swallowed hard. "Yeah," he repeated, and he lowered his eyes. He met Kenny's puzzled gaze. "Well, how's it look?" he asked, steeling himself for the worst.

Kenny let his breath out with a hiss. "Let's go into the back room," he said, turning abruptly.

Mike followed. Soon he found himself seated on a wooden crate, a cup of steaming black coffee in his hand, three of his former fellow workers surrounding him, listening to him explain what had happened today—and what he hoped to do.

"Supposing we do get you up to the orbital docks?" Kenny said finally. "What are you going to do? You don't have any papers, and you can't get work up there without them."

Mike glanced around, gauging the expressions on the faces of his old friends. "I'm going to try to work passage out," he said finally.

"Passage where? Mars? The asteroids?"

Mike shook his head and took a breath. "Out of the system. To Clypsis."

"*Clypsis?* The racing system?" Kenny shared his look of astonishment with his two coworkers.

"That's right. I'm going to find a way to sign on as an apprentice." Mike paused and looked at them, suddenly realizing how ridiculous that must sound. Clypsis was a fantasy; you didn't actually expect to *go* there. You just watched on the homeset and dreamed. He felt his own resolution harden in response to their obvious doubt, though he tried not to let it show on his face. He shrugged and took another bitter sip of coffee. "So," he said. "Do you think you can get me up to the docks?"

Kenny finally lowered his eyebrows. "I guess it'd be pretty rough on you to stay, huh?" Mike didn't answer. Finally Kenny nodded. "Well, there's a ship lifting from bay four at oh-five-hundred. Doug, you know the dispatch master better than I do. You think you can swing it for him?"

Doug, another tall, dark-haired young man, shrugged. "Can try."

"All right, you try, then. Mike, you gonna need anything else? You have a bag, anything, with you?"

Mike shook his head somberly and explained that he'd been unable to return to his home. He had no money to speak of, either, he admitted. "I have some savings, but if I try to make a withdrawal, it's bound to tip them off to where I am."

Kenny thought a moment. "All right. We'll see if we can do something about that, too. I think for now you'd better just sit tight here and let us try to pull the strings for you." He hesitated. "You're sure you want to do this? Once you leave, it won't be easy coming back..."

"I'm sure."

"Then, have some more coffee, and I think I can rustle you up a sandwich, too...."

Kenny appeared in the dark doorway, startling him. "Mike. There's a flight mech in bay four who'll get you on. Get over there now and ask for Tom."

Mike stood, stunned by the abruptness of the announcement. "Thanks," he said, a lump in his throat. He stuck out his hand.

Kenny shook hands—and pressed a small wad of bills into Mike's palm. Mike stared dumbly at the money before stammering, "I'll . . . I'll pay you back when I can."

"Don't worry about that," Kenny said. "It's not much, but it might help. Luck to you, babe. Maybe we'll be hearing about you in the racing reports one of these days."

"Yeah, maybe," Mike said hoarsely. Kenny clapped him on the back, and Doug and Rick appeared to say good-bye, and then he was outside in the damp, breezy night, walking across the tarmac. He walked quickly.

Launch-bay four loomed like a giant in the night: a complex of platforms and power-beam boosters and elevators and lights. The ship itself, a massive, flattened egg, was half-buried in the structure. Final loading procedures were being completed. Mike could see half a dozen or so human figures moving around the bay; he headed for the base of the structure and asked a dark-bearded man in silver coveralls where he might find Tom. The man scowled and pointed up.

Mike craned his neck and saw a blond-haired man leaning out over a catwalk, waving him up. "Level three!" he called.

Mike waved back and hurried to the nearest elevator. He stuck his hands in his pockets and drew a deep breath as the elevator lurched and took him up. As he stepped off on the third level, he tried to look confident.

Tom was waiting for him. "This way," he said, leading Mike in through one of the ship's side portals. They passed through a cargo hold and climbed a metal-runged ladder to a dimly-lighted crew deck crowded with grimy-looking consoles and three seats. The compartment smelled of ozone and stale air. In the far corner, practically hidden between a bulkhead and a cluster of conduit pipes, was a fourth seat. "That's your spot," Tom said. "We've got a man out sick on this trip—so it won't make any real difference to have you on board. If you sit there and keep quiet, nobody will mind."

Mike swallowed. "What if somebody asks me—"

"Tell them the Old Man's giving you a lift, and act like you belong here." Tom turned to leave. "I've got work to do, so you just strap in. They'll be lifting in two hours. The head's one deck up if you need it."

Mike nodded and squeezed himself past the bulkhead into the seat. Tom gave him a quick thumbs-up before disappearing back down the hatch. Resting his head back, Mike began the longest wait of his life.

CHAPTER 2

Lift-off came with a slam that told him instantly where the padding on his seat had been worn thin. Mike grimaced and tried to watch the nearest crewman, who was monitoring a console in apparent boredom. It put a crick in his neck to turn his head under acceleration, though; with an effort, he turned to peer forward again. And he thought: they were hurtling into space, and that man was *bored*! How could anyone be bored?

Still, as an exposed corner of the seat-frame gouged unrelentingly into his shoulder, with no hope of relief until the ground-based power beam cut off, the excitement began to pall—especially since he couldn't see a thing except a bulkhead shaking in front of him, or hear anything but a roar, not just behind, but all around him. He tried to imagine the view that the pilot and captain must have—a sunrise over the ocean, and a sky turning black.

The shaking subsided gradually, then cut off, and he felt himself rising against his straps. Seconds later, he was brought back down as the second power beam caught the ship—they must be high over the Atlantic now—and once more he was pinned to his seat, though with somewhat less force. At last, he could turn his head more easily to see the crewmen fiddling at their consoles. They'd been keeping a deliberately blind eye to his presence, but one man noticed him watching and winked.

Mike nodded and looked away. Soon they'd be in orbit, and from there it was just a brief coast to the docks.

* * *

It was actually four hours before Mike felt a series of thumps and heard someone call out, "Hard-docked." He'd had time to learn and be thankful that he seemed unsusceptible to microgravity sickness. But he'd not been out of his seat yet, either.

His chance came a few minutes later. He heard hatches being opened, and voices from the next deck, as the bridge began to empty. The nearest crewman hooked a thumb toward the cargo hold and mouthed the word *Go!* Hastily, Mike unbuckled and climbed out of his seat, moving awkwardly in the weightlessness. He pushed himself through the hatch into the cargo compartment, after one of the crewmen—and followed the man right out through the open portal, passing several dockworkers coming on board to begin supervising the unloading robots.

He found himself in a huge hangar area, where at least six ships were being serviced in a shirtsleeve environment; one wall of the hangar was a shimmering gray airscreen, bulging inward, where yet another small cargo shuttle was coming in. As he watched, the shuttle popped neatly through the forcefield and was towed to an empty bay. Mike blinked in wonderment, turned in midair, and grabbed a railing to continue on his way.

He'd lost sight now of the crewmen from his own ship, and he could only follow his instincts toward the exit. He kicked off toward the likeliest-looking cluster of people and hoped for the best.

The message was the third down on Officer Newman's screen when he arrived at the station first thing in the morning: *Approximately 0300, a young juvenile meeting description of one Mike Murray was observed at Canaveral Spaceport, approaching loading bays and possibly boarding an orbital cargo lifter, by a spaceport security agent who had not seen the bulletin regarding the missing youngster. Aforementioned youngster may have hitched ride to Capricorn Orbital Station. Ship lifted approximately 0505.*

Officer Newman grimaced at the news. The kid was quicker and more resourceful than Newman had given him credit for, if in fact it was Murray who the guard had seen. Newman's intuition suggested that it was. What a pain. Didn't the kid know that his aunt had an estate that had to be settled up, and that he would be coming into some money—not now, maybe, but when he turned eighteen?

With a sigh, Newman touched a button. "Forward this notice regarding runaway Michael MacAlister Murray to all spaceport authorities, including orbital ports. If Murray is found, he is to be put in touch with this office at once. Newman out."

He shook his head. It was likely to be days, anyway, before the notice was posted, and by then the kid would probably be long gone. So it went in this business. He shrugged. Putting the matter out of his mind, he went on to the next item on his screen.

The sign said CAPRICORN DOCKS CUSTOMS: ALL ARRIVING PARTIES. Mike stared at it for a moment and couldn't think of any alternative. He floated forward. The sign changed momentarily to CAUTION: GRAVITY AREA, and Mike steadied himself as his feet slowly came to the floor, and the sensation of weight returned to him. Less than Earth-normal, but adequate for comfort.

A blue-uniformed customs agent completed an inspection of someone else's bags and turned to Mike with raised eyebrows. Mike hesitated before putting his hand into the scanner. Would the police have a warrant out for his arrest? The machine read the ID chip implanted in his wrist, and a tiny green light flickered. "Baggage or cargo?" the customs agent asked. Mike shook his head. The eyebrows went up again, but the agent didn't comment, and instead motioned for Mike to step through a decontamination field. Mike breathed a sigh of relief. Apparently, at least, the police were not interested enough in him to have flagged the customs computers.

Emerging from the decon field, Mike faced the agent again. "Where are you staying?" the agent asked.

"I, uh—" Mike's voice caught. "Can you—suggest a place?"

"Sir, we cannot recommend any private establishment. However, the better housing is over in the second ring. If you're looking for something less expensive"—the agent stared at him appraisingly—"then you might try straight down corridor three to bottom level. It's cheaper down there." He bobbed his head toward the exit to indicate the direction.

Mike nodded. He was tempted to ask about work, but the man asked him first: "You have work papers? You can stay no more than seven days without showing papers."

"No, I—"

"Then, you've got to go to the registry. That's on level eight." The agent turned his head. "Next!"

Mike swallowed any other questions he might have had, and moved on. Passing out of the customs area, he came to a long, busy corridor, which curved upward out of sight both in front of him and behind. He was in one of the outer corridors that curved around the shell of the space station. Most of the people he saw looked like freight workers—mostly men, roughly dressed, talking and laughing in loud voices. The passenger area must be in another part of the station, if there was a passenger area.

He suddenly realized that he was starving. There ought to be some place around here to buy food—and come to think of it, some place with a window. Here he was in space, and he'd yet to see even the stars, much less Earth. Hurrying along, he found a ramp descending to a great concourse on a lower level. As he stepped off the ramp, he found himself in a crowded world of shops and coffee bars and liquor bars and holo-cinemas. The air was filled with the enticing smell of food, so much so that he found himself turning dizzily, unsure where to go first. The place reminded him of a games-park or a huge but dingy metropolitan airport.

His cash was limited, but he found a counter selling burga-rolls and coffee—for prices that took his breath away but at least were lower than in nearby cafes. The first bite of soymeat was so greasy he nearly gagged on it; however, hunger won out, and he wolfed the sandwich in about a minute and almost ordered another. Instead, he walked determinedly away, sipping his harsh coffee from a plastic cup.

For a time he just wandered, looking for a window. He didn't find one, but he did pass several bars with large videoscreens, and the thought struck him that perhaps he could catch some news or sports. Maybe he could catch some space-racing results from the Clypsis system: there were some results due in soon from a couple of the major races. Finally he worked up the nerve to go into one of the bars. Slipping quietly past the autotender, he took a seat in the corner, where he hoped he could watch the video undisturbed. The place was mostly deserted and the screen was indeed on a sports channel—showing results of collegiate free-fall soccer playoffs. The automatic bartender turned to gaze his way for a time, then rotated away. Mike held his breath and gazed up at the screen. "*. . . Hope you'll stay tuned for more soccer results, followed by the Downunder Cup light-sail preliminaries from Mars, and, of course, an update on the Five Star Jubilee race from the Clypsis system. The best in racing, here on WinLoss Central—*"

"Sonny . . ."

Mike jumped.

"This ain't no free video parlor." A middle-aged woman with purple-dyed hair and an irritated-looking expression had walked up behind him. "And we don't sell Shirley Temples. Are you looking to order something or not?"

"Well, I—no, I'm not—you see—"

"Right. Well, at least you didn't try to lie about your age." The woman sighed and hooked her thumb toward the exit. Mike let out his breath and glanced up longingly at the screen as he rose. They were showing a tantalizing glimpse of the racing news to come. "You want to watch? There's a pay-arcade three doors down," the woman said, jabbing again with her thumb. Mike nodded and took the hint.

It was actually seven doors down, and by the time Mike got there, he'd told himself that whatever it cost, it wasn't worth spending lunch money on. Then, walking by the arcade, he caught a glimpse of a screen and saw that they really were showing racing results. Damn. The Five Star Jubilee was a top-line race—the best of the best. He had to watch that one, at least to see who was winning . . .

He paid, wincing at the price, and ducked in to find a seat with a private screen. There was a split image on the screen, the left half showing current action—current, that is, at the moment of transmission from Clypsis; even by subspace, the transmission time was reckoned in days— while the right half of the screen gave a rundown of earlier races. Mike eagerly scanned the results, then scrutinized the displayed movements of spaceships in the star-system-wide racecourse.

Listed were the A-class through AAA-class stock races, the "workingman's" races, followed by the more prestigious classes one through three grand prix races, and, of course, the specials—the Five Star and its smaller cousins. The closest analog in ground-based racing to the specials, and actually a progenitor of the race, was the long-popular Indee 500 groundcar spectacular. As their names implied, these races used highly specialized space-ships in specific kinds of courses, and they tended to attract the best pilots and the latest and newest in racing technology. Mike modestly aspired to nothing less than one day racing in the Five Star Special himself; but, of course, he knew that he'd be incredibly lucky to fly even an A-class stock racer one day—or any other ship, for that matter.

On the left half of the screen now, the powerful Five Star ships were flashing around the sun of the Clypsis system at better than five times the speed of light. Mesmerizing images were streaming in from the racing web itself: the vast spiderweb-shaped system of warped-space channels through which the ships danced to the tune of danger and skill and the all-important wagers. A small display at the bottom of the screen offered Mike the chance to bet, if he so desired, to odds that changed moment by moment. Mike ignored it; he cared only for the racing, not for the gambling. The racers shot down the tubes of stressed space like blood cells spurting through arteries. Mike grew light-headed watching. His fingers tingled. He longed to be there so badly it hurt to watch. A racer named Sam Sams was in the lead. Mike didn't even care at this point who was winning; he just wanted to *be there*.

The image froze, and a winking light prompted him to approve an additional charge if he wanted to keep watching. Sighing, he rose. He couldn't afford it. But his eyes searched the room, trying to catch a glimpse on one of the other monitors. Instead, he saw the warning blinker of an automaton coming his way, no doubt to tell him to pay or leave. Mike shrugged and walked out. It's all crap until you get there in person, he told himself. Just concentrate on getting there.

He walked on, looking for a viewport. Eventually, he asked directions. A shop clerk told him how to get to the next-lower level, and finally he found a long series of observation windows. He tried to find one clean enough to see through. After rubbing a pane with his sleeve, he cupped his eyes to the glassite and peered out into space. What he could see was not much: a few vessels moving about near the docks . . . and *there,* barely visible at the bottom of the window, was the cloud-smudged rim of Earth. That was enough; it made his breath catch, and he swallowed with excitement and maybe just a touch of homesickness. It didn't change his resolve to leave, however.

He gazed a while, then started thinking about finding a place to sleep. By this time, he was having trouble standing with his eyes open; he'd been awake all night, at least as night was reckoned in Titus City. Here—well, he had no idea how the days were reckoned here, or whether there was such a thing as a night period or a day period, or whether everything just stayed in operation all the time.

He continued down the concourse. It wasn't long

before he found the place that the customs agent must have meant—a dingy sign over a large doorway: PUBLIC ROOMING. The advertised price was one he could just afford—and for no more than a few days, even if he didn't eat much. Inquiring within, he was directed down a grimy hallway by an old guy who took his money for a night's lodging, after making him pass his wrist through another ID scanner, and then returned to his scrutiny of a tattered hardcopy magazine. Mike shrugged and followed the hallway.

He found a large dormitory room, divided into sections by fabric tent-panels. Each panel surrounded a bunk; each had a number stenciled on the entry flap. A few men were walking to or from the lavatory, but no one spoke. Mike passed a guy sitting on his bunk with the tent flap open, unshaven chin in his hands, staring vacantly across the room. He probably didn't even see Mike pass. Mike found his number, used his wrist ID to get the flap open, and closed it behind him with a deep sigh before flopping down on the foam bunk.

Resting on his back, he folded his hands across his stomach and took several deep breaths, reflecting on what he was doing. He wondered if it made any sense at all. If he had known what these docks were like, would he have been so quick to flee Earth? This actually wasn't much worse than some of the homes he'd been placed in over the years—dirtier, maybe, but fundamentally not too different. At least here he was free to leave anytime he wanted . . . as soon as he had someplace to go . . . a job to take . . . a ship to join.

First thing in the morning, he would register. . . .

His eyes closed of their own accord, and he fell into a sound sleep.

Registering, he discovered, was easier said than done. He found the office after an hour's wandering and waited in line for what seemed like another hour. Everyone else in line was older than he. When he reached the front of the line, he found himself speaking to an automaton, which took his ID scan and hummed a moment before saying,

"You have an unclaimed message from Earth, Titus City Police Department, which you can claim at window six. Do you have any other business?"

"Yes, I want to register to work," Mike said. He glanced to the left and saw another long line at window six. Well, he had a pretty good idea what the message was, anyway. They wanted him to turn himself in. But probably they had no jurisdiction here.

"I can register you for food service or for delivery—"

"No. I mean, I want to ship out. I want a berth on a ship."

"That is impossible, until you reach the legal age of eighteen Earth years."

Mike flushed. "But—"

"That is the law," the automaton said.

"But surely there must be some way to—"

"I'm sorry, but there are other people waiting behind you. If you have no further business, please stand aside and let the next person approach."

Mike opened and closed his mouth several times, and finally stepped aside numbly. He'd expected his age to be a problem, but he'd just figured there *had* to be a way . . .

He felt a hand touch his shoulder. "Excuse me there, spaceman," he heard. He whirled.

Facing him was a stocky man—no, pudgy, he decided instantly and uncharitably—dressed in faded blue spacer clothes. The man had dark eyebrows and thinning black hair, and he wore smoked glasses. As he shifted his weight to gaze at Mike face to face, it was obvious that he moved with a limp. He regarded Mike through his dark lenses for a moment, while Mike tried to make up his mind whether he was a cop or a creep. "Couldn't help overhearing," the man said finally.

"Yeah?" Mike answered. He remembered now; he'd seen the man hanging around by the door.

"Yeah." The man scratched his nose. "Anyway, I guess you must have just gotten into town, or you'd know better than to try to register like this. What are you, fourteen? Fifteen?"

"Sixteen."

"Ah. Sixteen. A runaway?" The man raised a hand as he said it. "Whups—sorry. Don't tell me—I don't want to know."

Mike swallowed a sharp retort.

"Let's walk outside." The man gestured toward the door. "You want to collect your message first?"

Mike was irritated by the blatant treading on his privacy, but he looked at the line in front of the other window and shook his head. What was the point?

"All right . . . *Look, I'm not going to bite, kid*—I just thought I might be able to help."

"Yeah? What for?"

The man gazed at Mike, eyebrows raised. A smile played at the corner of his mouth. "Suspicious, aren't you? That's okay, it's a good trait—it might help keep you alive." The smile disappeared. "But that doesn't mean somebody can't be doing you a favor." The man shrugged. He was limping as they walked into the corridor. He turned and stuck out a finger at Mike's chest. "Look, I've been in your place, kid. I know what it's like. If you want to buck the system, it helps to know where it can be bucked and where it can't. Here at the registry . . ." He shrugged. "No way. But down on the docks is another story."

Mike was silent.

"You want to ship out?" the man asked. He waited for an answer.

Mike finally nodded grudgingly.

"All right, then. Forget registry. Go down to the hangars. There are plenty of ships that could use an extra hand, if you're willing to work for a little less than scale."

"Just like that? Just walk around and say, 'Hey—'?"

"You want a name? I can give you a name."

"I—well—"

The man's finger pointed at him again. "Josiah Bent. Can you remember that? Josiah Bent. He's a skipper, and I'll bet he can use you. Is it worth a try?"

Mike opened his mouth.

Pointing down the corridor, the man said, "See that lift-tube? Take it to dock-level. Then turn left when you come out and walk out to hangar thirty-one-B. You'll find a ship there called the *Swamp Queen*. Just ask for Captain Bent, and if he wants to know how you found out about him, you tell him Slippery Gene sent you." He smiled, in reaction to Mike's suspicious look. "Don't worry about it, kid. It's just a nickname."

Mike nodded, at a loss.

"Think you can find it? I'd go down with you myself, but I figure you might like to find your own way. And I've got other fish to fry, anyway."

"Well—thanks." Mike flushed.

"Don't mention it, kid. Good luck." Gene clapped him on the arm and limped away.

Mike stood rocking on the balls of his feet for a few moments, then clucked his tongue and sauntered in the general direction Gene had indicated. He wasn't anxious to take unsolicited advice from a stranger. On the other hand, did he have a better idea?

Without actually making a conscious decision to do so, he eventually made his way toward the dock level and hangar 31B, after a detour for sight-seeing and a snack. The snack forced him to take stock of his cash situation, and after that, he moved toward the dock with greater urgency.

Hangar 31B was in the seediest-looking part of the docks. Entering the hangar nervously, he looked out from a catwalk over a cluster of freighters, none of them very spaceworthy-looking. He inspected them from a distance, trying to make out their names. Several of them were large and black and ungainly. He couldn't decipher their names, but that, he decided, was because they were in an alien script. His judgment was confirmed as he saw several crewmembers emerge from one of the ships; they wore protective suits, were headless, and had too many limbs. He watched them move around their ships for a time before turning his attention to the other vessels.

One was noticeably more battered-looking than the

others; it was smaller and squatter, and it had a scarred gray finish—if it could be called a finish—that looked as though it had passed through too many dust-hazard clouds. A sinking feeling in Mike's stomach matched his sudden intuition that that was, in fact, the *Swamp Queen*. Well, he thought, the situation could probably be worse. He hoped.

Descending from the walkway, he stepped onto the hangar floor—and felt the floor fall away as he floated into the air. Microgravity again—this time without a warning sign. He tumbled head over heels once, then managed to catch a railing and stabilize himself before pushing off in a controlled fashion. He sailed across the floor, touched, and kicked off again, grateful for his school gymnastics training, and finally landed near the base of the ship. He read in faded letters near the main portal: *Swamp Queen*. Taking a breath, he approached the portal.

"Who you lookin' for, there, bub?" he heard, as he was about to step through the open hatch.

He turned and saw a stubble-faced man in a charcoal-gray jumpsuit swing around a stabilizer to land beside him. The man was breathing with a rasp; his eyes flashed blue as he scrutinized Mike.

"Josiah—ah, I mean, *Captain* Josiah Bent," Mike said. "Is that you?"

The man squinted. "Not hardly, no. I'm Bowker Ferguson, First Mate. What'd you want to see the skip' about?"

"I, ah—well—I thought he might—need another hand," Mike mumbled. There was something intimidating about this Bowker Ferguson; he looked like someone you might not want to cross.

"Mmm. You want to sign on, you're sayin'?" Ferguson grinned, displaying a set of crooked teeth. "Okay, come on, and I'll see if the cap' can talk to you. What d'ya know how to do?"

"Ah—well"—Mike blushed—"I've studied piloting and some programmed fusion engineering, and—"

Ferguson's grin widened. "Sounds good. What's your name?"

25

"Mike Murray."

"Okay, Mike Murray. Come on aboard."

Captain Josiah Bent was a fat, olive-skinned man in his forties, Mike guessed, who looked like he'd always been on a spaceship and always would be. His eyebrows quivered as he heard Mike out on why he was here—and when Mike mentioned the name of Slippery Gene, he nodded knowingly, eyebrows dancing. "So," he said, "you want to see the stars, and you've got no papers. You're a fugitive from Earthside law, and you're—I would guess to look at you—underage. Anything else you want to tell me?" He pushed back in his seat, puffing on an enormous pipe.

"I've—studied piloting and fusion—" Mike began.

"Where, on a computer sim?"

"Yes, I—"

Bent waved him silent. Mike could scarcely breathe; the captain's quarters were claustrophobically small to begin with, and were littered with papers and books and uniform coats secured with loose bungee cords. The pipe smoke curled about the ceiling ventilation grill and blew back toward the center of the room.

"Well," Bent said, "we'll see. Look, we don't stand too much on formality on this ship. You look like a bright kid, and you've got spunk, so if you're willing to work hard, I think we can use you. You'll be grunt-class at first, of course, but you'll get to see the stars." He exhaled a cloud of reeking smoke and said, "Tell Fergie to show you down to the crew's quarters and get you settled in." Bent suddenly lurched out of his seat, and Mike floated hastily out of the way of his bulk. Bent opened the cabin door. "Fergie!" he bellowed.

"Here, skipper," a voice echoed.

"Show Spaceman Murray to his quarters!" Bent turned to Mike. "Get settled in, son. We hit space in twelve hours."

Mike had enough time to get acquainted with the layout of the ship and meet a few of his crewmates, and

still go back to the dock mall to buy a change of clothes—
there were no such niceties as uniforms on the *Swamp
Queen*—and a few bags of Georgia maca-nuts, all at
extortionate prices, and to send a postgram to his friends at
the Canaveral Spaceport, telling them of his good luck.
Next stop, Eridani 'Twixt, he wrote. *It's not Clypsis, but
it's almost in the right direction. Keep your fingers crossed.
And thanks.* He hesitated a moment before sending it, then
decided that if he'd escaped flagging on the computers so
far, it was unlikely that postgrams were being screened.
He pushed the button.

Finally he spent a little time wandering around the
station. He found an observation area with clean windows and a spectacular view of Earth, the Moon, and
the stars. He lingered there a little while, trying to pick
out familiar features, and trying to summon the courage
to face up to what he was about to do. He might never
see his homeworld again. Eventually he simply turned
away and fled back down to the dock area and reboarded
the *Swamp Queen*.

Settling into his berth, he waited for departure.

Earth dwindled in the galley monitor, becoming a
blue-green dot against the darkness of the solar system.
Mike glanced at the screen between trips from the grill to
the tiny dining area. His main job was helping the cook, or
anyone else who needed help, though Captain Bent had
hinted that they might check him out on the computer
systems a little later. Though he had scant time to dwell on
the view, he couldn't help being struck by what a stagger-
ing amount of the solar system was emptiness. They had to
travel out beyond the orbit of Mars before the shift into
subspace, and they were all getting an eyeful of emptiness.

When he wasn't cleaning up in the galley, he was
cleaning tools and panels belowdecks. It was hard, tedious
work, but it suited him well enough. He was eating, and
he had a place to sleep, and he was going where he wanted
to go, more or less.

A week out of Earth orbit, the warning came over the

intercom: "Make ready for shift to subspace! All hands make ready!"

Strapped into his bunk, Mike exchanged thumbs-up gestures with two other crewmen, and then he closed his eyes as the words, "Shifting now!" echoed in the corridors.

The ship, and the universe, turned inside out.

CHAPTER 3

Life aboard a freighter was both duller and more exciting than Mike had expected. Time passed slowly during transit, but Mike welcomed the opportunity to learn firsthand about life in space—the duties, the skills required, the tedium. The *Swamp Queen* was not exactly the lap of luxury, and he often wondered if its life-support systems and space drive were any more reliable than the facilities for creature comforts. The compartments were always either too hot or too cold, the cooking equipment was temperamental at best, and—three times in the first week—Mike was called upon to hold tools for the chief engineer, Mary-All Dridge, while she repaired the gravity generator.

The crew were all human; three men and three women. They seemed to accept him readily enough as one of them, though he came in for some teasing once they got wind of his ambitions to go to Clypsis to become a racer. He never could figure out where, or if, the joke left off and the derision began, but he kept a stone-face whenever the subject arose, and pretended not to take their jokes seriously.

Until their first stop, a brief layover at Eridani 'Twixt where he didn't even get to leave the ship, Mike kept his nose clean and didn't ask much about the *Swamp Queen*'s cargo; but on the second leg of the flight, he started trying in earnest to learn just what it was that they carried. The crew became very quiet when he raised the subject. What had piqued his curiosity was the revelation that the ship's name had been changed: *Swamp Queen* was now *Steam*

Heat, and had been since three days out of Eridani 'Twixt, when two crewmen had gone outside to perform maintenance on the hull. They'd returned bearing long, thin strips of metal carrying the ship's name and registry numbers, having just replaced the old name and numbers with the new ones.

Mike hadn't said anything right away, but he found the change troubling. Were they up to something illegal? A crewman named Craig Show, a big fellow who was usually full of belly laughs, finally sat down somberly and clued him in. "It's not exactly within the letter of the law," he admitted. "I guess you've figured that out already. The cap' doesn't really want us to talk about it, but has the word *smuggling* crossed your mind?"

Mike stared at him, not answering. No doubt he'd been naive; but he'd sort of, in the back of his mind, been hoping to hear something else. He swallowed. Wake up, kid. It's the real world.

"You look shocked," said another crewmember, a young woman named Dixie Jewell. "Don't you know how many of the big racers got their starts smuggling contraband into the outworld systems?"

"Yeah, I guess so," Mike said slowly. Somehow, though, hearing about others doing it was different from doing it himself. Smuggling, after all, was illegal; and if it meant carrying drugs, or guns, or something . . . Well, he didn't exactly have it worked out in his head, but he knew it gave him an uneasy feeling in his belly.

Craig seemed to read his thoughts. "It's not as bad as what you're thinking."

Mike looked at him questioningly.

Craig sighed and rose to close the compartment door.

"Craig . . ." Dixie warned.

Craig waved off the objection. "He's one of us now, right? Look. We're not really supposed to tell you. So you didn't hear it from us, okay?"

"Sure."

"All right, then. We just dropped off some organic

computer nodules at 'Twixt, and now we've got some superfilament for Dylstra. It's that kind of stuff.''

Mike looked from Craig to Dixie and back. "I don't get it. Why should that kind of stuff *need* to be smuggled?''

It was Dixie Jewell who answered. "You have any idea how much that kind of thing gets *taxed* some places?''

Mike shook his head.

"Plenty," Craig said. "On a lot of worlds, people can't even get stuff like that. Now, sometimes it's just because the government's milking the trade, but other places—Dylstra, for instance—they tax certain valuable items to death to keep supplies limited. So prices stay up, and only the ruling class can lay their hands on the stuff.'' He frowned, rubbing his ear. "So there's an under-the-table market. And that's where we come in.''

For a moment, Mike didn't answer. He couldn't help thinking that probably it was smugglers who'd let the beajangles onto Earth, and if it hadn't been for the beajangles, his aunt would still be alive.

"I don't mind saying we're pretty good at it," Craig added.

Mike blew between his hands, nodding. He guessed it wasn't the worst thing in the universe, but . . .

Before he could say anything more, a call crackled over the intercom: "Mike Murray to the bridge, please. Mike Murray to the bridge.''

It was the navigator who wanted to see him. Vicky Slicky, they called her. She was a tough old bird (not really *that* old), but everyone seemed to think she was also the best navigator in the greater Orion arm of the Milky Way galaxy. The only time she'd ever talked to Mike before had been to bawl him out for not cleaning and calibrating the parallax-scope before their approach to Eridani 'Twixt, when in fact he'd had not the slightest idea that such a thing was supposed to be done.

Mike approached with some trepidation. Vicky looked up sharply, like an eagle with a rabbit in its sights. "Did you . . . want to see me?" he asked cautiously.

31

"What took you so long?"

"Excuse me?" he asked in bewilderment.

"Next time I call, I want you here in thirty seconds, not a second more. I have no time to waste. Now, shall we get on with your lesson?"

Mike opened his mouth. Lesson?

"You wanted to learn the computer system, didn't you? You're supposed to be some kind of hotshot kid with a computer."

"Well, I—I mean, on simulations, I—"

"Sit down." She slapped the chair in front of the main console.

Mike obeyed, sweating. He was painfully conscious of the captain watching. Josiah Bent was perched silently in his seat overlooking the rest of the tiny bridge, and just now the only person he had to watch was Mike. He gave no sign of concern; he just puffed his pipe calmly, filling the room with a dizzying reek of smoke. Mike struggled to concentrate on what Vicky was saying.

"Here's how we store the navigational charts," she said, touching several glowing spots in rapid sequence, "and here are the logs and flight records"—and as she spoke, several screens lighted with text and geometric charts—"and now here's the processing area for calculating the subspace translations . . ."

Mike listened carefully, trying to understand what she was saying in terms of the mechanics he'd already studied at home. He obeyed her instructions as she led him through some sample calculations; and before he knew it, three hours were gone, and his head hurt, but he had just completed a simulated jump from Alpha Centauri to Sirius B.

"I'm stunned," Vicky Slicky said quietly, staring at the results.

He frowned. "Did I get it right?"

"No," she said, pointing to the screen. "You did this transform wrong. But you did *this* transform right. On the first try. Either you're very lucky, or you have talent, after all."

Mike grinned and turned to catch the captain's reaction. Bent was in the process of relighting his pipe. He looked as though he hadn't stirred in the three hours, or noticed a thing. He puffed his pipe, and gazed at the blank viewscreen, and gazed blankly at Mike. Mike turned back as Vicky said, "Enough for today. Be back here same time tomorrow. I think they need you in the galley now. . . ."

By the time of their approach to Yolaan's World, Mike had worked up to a fair proficiency with the navigational computer—though he was still spending the majority of his duty hours belowdecks, scrubbing tables in the galley or helping Mary-All in the engineering compartment. He was looking forward to planetfall; being aboard ship was well and good, but he was starting to long for an open sky and a breath of unrecirculated air. He voiced his thoughts to Mary-All one day, and she looked up from the circuit cube she was testing and said, dark eyes peering at him in puzzlement, "We're only going to be docking in orbit, you know—and only for a few hours. We won't be planetside at all."

Mike blinked. Somehow he'd forgotten, in his wishful thinking—but of course he'd known that. He was, he hated to admit, just a bit homesick for Earth. For clouds, and trees, and sunshine. Was this the price he had to pay for his choice? Never to see these things again?

"Don't worry," Mary-All said, sensing his reaction. "A few more stops, and the captain will probably put in somewhere and give us shore leave. He's a smart man. He knows he can't keep us cooped up forever, not without having morale go all to hell."

"Yeah," Mike murmured, thinking of his plans to get to Clypsis, and wondering how he was going to manage that, since he'd already learned that Clypsis was not on the *Swamp Queen*'s—or rather, *Steam Heat*'s—itinerary.

"Oh, I forgot," Mary-All said, raising her eyebrows. "You're going to leave us to go fly on those crazy racers, and probably blow yourself to kingdom come, in the bargain." Mike blushed, but she went on, saying, "Why don't you just stay with us and make a nice honest living in the freight business? Good benefits, and a great future.'' She winked knowingly and returned to her work, and Mike walked out of the compartment feeling slightly dazed.

Fortunately, the business of bringing the ship in to the Yolaan's World orbital docks took his mind off the problem soon enough. Mike was allowed on the bridge for the actual approach this time—watching over Vicky Slicky's shoulder as she figured the orbits and transferred the data to Bowker Ferguson, who was doing the actual piloting. "How fas' kin I bring her in, Cap'?" Fergie asked, with an exaggerated wink at Mike. "Mind if I take a crack at breakin' that ol' track record?"

Vicky Slicky scowled without looking at the mate, but the captain answered. "If this ship were your dear old gram's, and she had no insurance—that's how fast you may bring her in," he said, looking at no one in particular. For once, his pipe was not in his hand.

Mike silently wished they'd all knock it off. But with the docking station coming up in the viewscreen, he forgot everything except the figures and shapes swelling up on the nav screens, and the languid motions of the pilot making small, seemingly careless adjustments to the ship's course. Mike felt himself transported back to the computer simulations he'd run a hundred times back in Titus City; he almost felt himself becoming one with the ship's guidance control. The station was growing large now, and the adjustments more critical . . . he wished he could just put his hands on the controls, in place of Fergie's . . .

Minutes later, they were hard-docked, and the mate and navigator were securing the bridge, as Captain Bent announced a four-hour liberty to the crew.

The name of the place was Stemple's Saloon. It was really more of a cafe than a saloon, but Mike liked the name; as long as he wasn't old enough to be legal, at least he could preserve his dignity as a spacer by sitting here sipping a drink—which just happened to be the local soft drink, something made from roots and herbs. The rest of the crew had scattered, mostly to real watering holes, or heaven-knew-where-else; but Mike was content to be alone for a while, to just sit and stare out the window—a *clean* window, too—at the swirling mists of Yolaan's World. He wondered what sort of world it was down there, whether it was hot or cold, what the people were like. He wondered if it might be a place he'd enjoy visiting.

"Can I get you something else?"

Mike turned his head. A young woman with short-cut blond hair and a friendly smile had approached his table. Her nametag identified her as "Jayne." When he didn't answer immediately, she laughed and said, "That's okay. You're allowed to just enjoy the view. Where are you from?" Mike told her. Her face lit up. "*Earth?* I've wanted all my life to go to Earth." She glanced around the room; it was half empty. Apparently satisfied that no other customers required her attention, she said, "Do you mind if I sit down a minute?"

Mike shrugged, grinning. She slid into the opposite seat. "Now, tell me all about it," she said. He opened his mouth, and nothing came out. She laughed explosively. "Okay, just tell me about"—she thought a moment— "*Africa*. What's Africa like?"

He blinked rapidly. "Well, I . . . I don't know. You see, I've . . . I've never been—"

"America, then?" she pleaded.

He finally joined her in laughter, and began telling her where he'd lived, in Ohio and Florida. After a few minutes, she had to get up to serve some other customers. Mike's gaze followed her as she scurried around the room. A man sat down at the next table, and Jayne took his order. As she left his table, the man's eyes caught Mike's for a moment before he turned to glance out the window.

After a few quick trips about the room, Jayne returned. "Okay," she said. "Tell me more about Florida. And how'd you get here? You seem—excuse me, but you seem a little young to be traveling on your own."

Mike blushed. He wished people would stop harping on his age. Immediately Jayne looked apologetic, though, so he shrugged and told her a bit about how he'd left Earth, and why. "I came in on the *Swamp Queen*," he said—and then, remembering a heartbeat too late, he amended that by saying, "I mean, uh, *Steam Heat*." When she looked puzzled, he added lamely, "*Swamp Queen* was another ship." Over her shoulder, he saw the man at the next table staring at him, and their eyes locked together for an uncomfortable instant. Mike felt the blood rise in his face. He wasn't supposed to mention the ship's name while he was ashore, he remembered; and he certainly wasn't supposed to have let slip her original name. The man nodded as though to himself and looked away. Mike shifted his gaze back to Jayne, wondering what the guy might have heard. "So," he said. "Are you from the planet?"

She chuckled. "The planet? You make it sound like a prison or something. Yes, I'm from Yolaan's. I'm working my way—What? Is something wrong?"

The man at the next table had just gotten up and walked out. "Uh . . . that guy left without waiting for his order," he said, tilting his head.

Jayne turned to look. "Rrrr. Those customs people. They always act like they own the place, and then—*hey, where are you going?*"

Rising dizzily, Mike whispered, "I . . . have to leave now." *Customs people?* What had he done?

She rose with him, looking concerned. "Are you all right? You look pale."

"Yes, uh—yes. I have to go now." He started for the door, then remembered that he hadn't paid. He dug into his pocket and put some money on the table without counting it. "I'm sorry," he said with a grimace.

"Wait—you don't owe that much. Wait!"

But he was already out the door, hurrying toward the docks as fast as he could walk.

"What are you doing here?" Captain Bent said, looking up as Mike sailed onto the ship's bridge. Gravity was off while they were docked.

36

"Customs!" Mike gasped. "Might be coming! Are the nameplates hidden? . . . flight logs?"

Bent looked at him as if he were crazy. "What are you talking about?" he demanded. He put his pipe down and rose out of his seat. "What's this about customs?"

Breathlessly, Mike stammered out an explanation of his slip at the cafe. "I'm . . . I'm not sure he heard me . . . but the waitress said he was customs, and . . ." He paused and gulped some air. "The man left . . ."

"All right, now, calm down," Bent said. "Get in that seat." He motioned to the navigator's seat, and Mike sat. "Now, it's probably nothing. We can't just go flying off in a panic because some customs agent might suspect something." He frowned, thinking. "Still . . ."

Mike cleared his throat. "Do . . . do they know . . . I mean, the *Swamp Queen?*"

Bent's gaze flickered onto him. "What? Yes, of course, why do you think we—" His eyes flashed suddenly. "Say, how much do you know about this, anyway, young Mr. Murray?"

"I—well—" Mike felt his face grow red.

"*Damn,* won't this crew ever learn to keep their mouths shut?" Bent sighed. "Well, it's no good taking chances, even though the cargo's already off." He clicked the intercom. "Mary-All, are you back on board? Vicky? *Anyone?*" There was no answer. "Damn. All right, lad, I guess it's up to the two of us." He pursed his lips and checked the outside monitors. "Uh-oh. We're bejoogered now. Here comes the customs squad."

Mike leaned and saw an image of three uniformed men crossing the hangar area toward the ship. He looked up at Bent worriedly. "What are we going to—"

"Bless me!" Bent exclaimed. "I haven't used that computer in years! Do you know how to bleed off those logs in a hurry? Anything that has *Swamp Queen* or our old registry number on it?"

"Why, yes, I think I—"

Mike's answer was interrupted by a squawk from the console: "*This is Customs Control to* Steam Heat. *We have a Section Five-ninety directive, restraining you from departure until your ship and flight records have been examined. Please respond."*

"Do it!" Bent snapped, pounding his fist into his hand. "We can play dumb for a minute or two. Restraining us from departure. Hah! How can I depart without my crew, anyway, eh? Don't erase anything labeled *Steam Heat*—we have to have a history to show, you know."

Mike didn't answer; he was already busy at the navigational console, picking his way through the files. It was a good thing he'd spent some time at this already, because Vicky had it set up in a peculiarly convoluted format, and there was no easy way to delete incriminating entries in a hurry.

"Keep at it," Bent said. He clicked the communication set. "Ah, this be *Steam Heat*. Please to repeat that last message, please?" He clicked off the sender and checked the outside monitors. "How are you doing?" he asked Mike. "I figure you have about one more minute before they board. I hope Mary-All stored those nameplates like she was supposed to."

Mike let out a breath, trying not to be distracted. Could he do it in a minute? He'd raced time on computers before. For a moment, he blanked; and then it was as though his time sense shifted, as though the world around him slowed, as he sank into a state of heightened sensitivity and reflex (this was how racing pilots did it, he'd always thought; it was this ability to sink into a dreamstate of speed that had made him think he could become a racer); and he realized that he was merely *thinking* about doing it quickly . . . and then the image of how to do what needed to be done leaped from his mind straight to his fingertips . . .

. . . and in a few seconds, his breath escaped in a long, painful sigh. He drew another breath and gazed at the log record and realized that somehow, *somehow,* he'd actually brought forth the reflexes and the insight, and he'd *done it*. The log was clear. He looked up at the captain, blinking. "Done," he whispered.

At that moment, he heard a commotion outside—

Bowker Ferguson arguing with the customs men. Bent grabbed Mike by the collar and practically hurled him off the bridge, hissing, "Get below. And if they ask you, my name is Ess. Captain Charles Ess. Got that?"

Mike hurried below, repeating to himself, "Captain Ess, Captain Charles Ess. . . ."

The customs agents moved noisily through the ship. Mike, in his bunkspace, could hear someone arguing with the captain in the corridor. Their voices faded in the direction of the bridge, but Mike could hear Fergie yelling at the others to be careful as they went down into the cargo hold. After a time, they came back up through the crew quarters, banging doors as they went. Mike's bunkspace door flew open, and a stranger stared in at him. The stranger hooked his thumb in a gesture to come out.

"What's goin' on?" Mike murmured. "Where's Cap'n Ess?" He kicked off ahead of the man down the passageway.

"We'll do the asking. You the kid who was talking about a ship called the *Swamp Queen*?" the man said, when Mike faced him again in the galley.

Mike looked at him twitchily. "Huh?"

"*Were you talking about the* Swamp Queen?" the man repeated savagely.

"Hey, now—there's no call to be shouting at the young lad that way!" The captain floated in, followed by another agent. He shook a finger at the agent.

The stranger ignored the interruption. "Answer the question," he said.

Mike looked wide-eyed at him. "I've heard of a ship by that name."

"And what do you know about it?" the agent demanded.

Mike trembled. "I . . . don't . . ." He shrugged nervously. "I just heard of it, that's all. Cap'n Ess, what's this all about?"

Before the captain could answer, the other agent said, "Never mind. Come on, Harry. There's nothing on the bridge, and they need us back at the office. Where's Joe?" The two agents kicked out of the galley and were joined by the third in the passageway. They disappeared toward the portal.

A minute later, Fergie joined Mike and the captain in the galley. "They're gone," he said. *"What happened?"*

Mike swallowed and turned toward the captain, prepared for the reprimand that was almost certain to come. He was startled to see, instead, a broad grin spreading across the captain's face.

CHAPTER 4

"**G**ood show!" the captain crowed, and promptly sent Mike down into the holds along with Fergie, while he himself disappeared back onto the bridge. There was no time to talk about it just then, but Mike left with the distinct impression that the captain had *enjoyed* the episode.

By the time he came back up on deck, the rest of the crew had returned. When the restraining order against departure was lifted by a disgruntled customs office—perhaps (Mike suspected) encouraged by a well-placed bribe or two—the captain wasted no time in making for open space. It wasn't until they were well clear of Yolaan's World, though, that the crew found time to gather around the galley and discuss what had happened. Mike, instead of being bawled out for his mistake, found himself receiving congratulations for his fast thinking. He found the whole thing a trifle unsettling.

The captain had been seen whistling with uncharacteristically good cheer, and the last time Mike had stepped onto the bridge, he'd been greeted with a booming hello. "We all need a good vitamin charge once in a while," the captain had said, as though that explained it.

Mike, joining the others, answered some questions and asked a few of his own. "Where *did* you hide those nameplates, anyway?" he asked Mary-All in bewilderment. The customs agents had not found a thing.

The engineer was grinning too widely to speak. Craig

41

Show answered for her. "They were inside the baffles of the fusion reactor. That's where we keep them all."

"All?" Mike asked numbly.

"Yeah, we have—what?—four sets of plates? Or are we up to five now?" Craig asked Dixie. "They're a little hot now; we have to be pretty careful taking them out of there."

"We're back down to four, since the skipper dropped *Bluejay of Paradise*," Dixie said. She looked at Mike. "What amazes me is that the skip' wasn't even mad at you. When *I* pulled a boner like that once, I was in the doghouse for weeks. I don't get it."

"Well, when you pulled yours," Craig said, laughing, "you didn't get us out of it. Skipper had to do that himself. Now, to hear Vicky Slick' talk about it, Mike pulled off a pretty good feat with her computer. This kid's going to make quite a racer, if he ever makes it to Clypsis."

Mike blushed. It had turned out that Vicky'd had an automatic-erasure program built into the log files for just such an emergency; but since he hadn't known about it, he'd done the whole thing the hard way—which Vicky'd said later was nigh unto impossible, at least in that short a time. She'd credited it to Mike's youth, and the time he'd spent with computers in his self-teaching programs; in fact, she'd recommended to Captain Bent (or Ess, which was what everyone was calling him now) that he give Mike a bonus for a job well done.

And yet . . . though he was apparently the hero, Mike couldn't help feeling troubled. These people were his friends, and heaven knew he was no angel. And yet . . .

Smuggling was smuggling, and no matter how many of the racers in Clypsis had started their careers that way, it was still against the law, and it sometimes hurt people. His aunt, for instance—or victims of illegal drugs, or weapons.

"Hey, why the long face?" Dixie asked him.

He started and smiled weakly. "Guess I'm just beat," he said. "It's been a long day."

42

"Well, why don't you go hit the sack? We'll clean up in here."

"Thanks," Mike said, rising. He looked around the galley and forced a grin. "Wake me if anything exciting happens," he joked, then turned and headed for his bunkspace.

It was two days into the subspace passage that Captain Bent, or Ess, called him to his quarters. "Ah, it's you," the captain said, absently waving away a cloud of smoke that was encircling his head. "Here." He tossed Mike an envelope. Mike caught it and looked at it in puzzlement. "Go ahead, open it." Mike did, and found in it six crisp interstellar-yen notes. Mike fingered them wonderingly for a moment, then looked up. "That's your pay, plus bonus," the captain said. "Consider it a severance bonus."

"But—" Mike's voice caught. "Severance?"

"Let's just say that your trial period is over. You want to stay on board, you have to do it under new terms." Bent/Ess paused to relight his pipe, not looking at him.

Mike was speechless.

"You have to take double the pay, and twice the responsibility," the captain added carelessly.

Mike's mouth opened. "You mean, I'm—"

"Not grunt-class anymore. That's right. You're a full-fledged member of the crew—with, ah, all of the first-class prerogatives that accompany that honor, as soon as we think of some. Welcome aboard, son!" The captain blew a great puff of pungent smoke.

Mike could think of nothing to say. He finally swallowed, and folded the money and slipped it into his pocket. "Thank you," he said softly. "But I—"

"But *what?*" Bent/Ess asked. He waved a hand in dismissal. "No buts. You're on board, and you're now officially the assistant to the navigator. You still have to take the regular rotation of galley and maintenance duty, but no more than anyone else. Fergie will fill you in." The captain's eyes closed, then opened again. "Now scram, while I put the word out."

Mike nodded and swallowed again, and with a clumsy salute turned to leave. On his way below to the bunkspace area, he heard the intercom crackle to life, and the captain's voice announcing to all decks that one Mike Murray had just joined the crew with full rank and privilege. Mike stopped in his bunk area before going to the galley, and sat on his bunk shaking his head, and wondered: What am I going to do now?

"Hey, Mike. You look like you lost your heart back on Yolaan's World. What's wrong?"

Mike looked up. Mary-All crossed the galley and drew herself a cup of tea. He shrugged.

"Come on, now—you've been looking that way since the skipper announced that you were—" Mary-All suddenly fell silent. "Oh," she said. "You weren't going to—" She cut herself off again and nodded.

Mike looked at her silently.

She slid her cup along the table and sat across from him. Her dark fingers plucked at curly hair. Her mouth pursed. "So, what are you going to do?" she said finally.

Mike looked at the tabletop. He pushed around a breadcrumb with his finger for a minute before answering. "Well, Dylstra is as close as we're going to Clypsis, according to the flight plan. I was planning to tell the skipper that I wanted to get off there, but . . ." Mike struggled for words. "He didn't really let me talk. I guess now I'll just have to jump—"

Mary-All put a finger to her lips, cutting him off. She shook her head. *Don't say it,* she mouthed. Mike looked at her in puzzlement, until she leaned forward and whispered, "The walls have ears, and the skipper wouldn't like to hear that." Mike made a gesture of helplessness. She hesitated, then murmured, "Don't panic. There may be something we can do." Mike's eyes widened, and she raised a cautioning finger. "*May* be."

"What?" he whispered.

44

Mary-All looked thoughtful. "I'm not sure. But give me a little time." Mike sighed impatiently. Her gaze sharpened. "I mean it, Mike. Trust us. Be patient."

He gave in and nodded. What choice did he have?

As the days wore on through the approach to Dylstra, he began to realize just how dependent he was on the goodwill of his crewmates. He knew full well that his plans to go to Clypsis could be a pipe dream—in fact, he'd been so busy with his duties here, and learning practical navigation from Vicky, that he'd hardly had time to think about racing at all. But one thing he did know: he didn't want to make a career of being a smuggler.

It only made matters worse that he'd gotten so much credit for pulling them out of trouble on Yolaan's World, and that he'd gotten a promotion to boot; it made it that much harder to contemplate leaving—especially since the captain had made such a point of his new status on the ship. Any time the subject of racing came up on the bridge, the captain cut it off; and he always seemed to be going on now about the scarcity of such promising recruits as Mike.

Mike was flattered but puzzled. Did the captain really think he was such a whiz—or was this just a way of keeping him on the hook? Vicky Slicky was treating him more respectfully nowadays—and more demandingly—but Vicky seemed to remain aloof from the captain's whims and moods, so her attitude toward Mike probably wasn't much of a guide.

If only he could *talk* to the captain, Mike thought; but both Mary-All and Craig had cautioned against it. The captain, Mary-All said, could be a peach as long as you were on his good side. But if you got him angry, watch out.

And it would surely make him angry to hear that Mike was leaving.

About all he could do was wait—and hope that the others could come through for him.

He trusted their promise. But waiting was hard.

* * *

It was on the day of their arrival at Dylstra that Mary-All took him aside on the engineering deck. "I have to be back on the bridge in five minutes," Mike said worriedly as she led him over near the noisiest pump on the deck.

"Do you still want to go?" she asked, her voice nearly drowned out by the screech of a failed bearing. Mike winced at the sound, and she grinned. "Gonna have to fix this thing," she shouted. "*After* we dock." Mike nodded, and she repeated her question. "Do you still want to go?"

He swallowed. "Of course!"

"Are you sure? You aren't going to change your mind?"

He gazed at her and tried to pretend that his heart wasn't pounding. "I'm sure," he answered.

She nodded, eyes closing, then reopening. "All right. Here's what we're going to do. Craig has some friends on the Dylstra station. We think they can help. Now, the problem is that the cap' will be watching you like a hawk to make sure you don't leave the ship. So this is what we need you to do . . ."

Mike leaned close and listened. When she was finished, he said, "Okay, but . . ."

"But what?"

His mouth opened before he found the words. She gestured impatiently. "Well . . . isn't this going to get *you* in trouble with the captain? You and Craig and Dixie?"

Mary-All gazed at him intently for a moment, then smiled. "Well, let's just say"—her voice was nearly inaudible over the pump—"that we like to gamble, too. Just like the captain. Why do you think he was so happy when we left Yolaan's? It's because he almost got caught— *and didn't*. So don't worry about us, okay?"

Mike nodded and couldn't say anything more then, because Mary-All had him by the arm and was propelling him toward the door. "See you when we're docked," she said. And then he was alone in the corridor.

As he made his way back to the bridge, he tried to ignore the knot in his stomach. It wasn't fear this time, though. It was sadness. After all this, no matter how it came out, he was going to miss his good friends.

"Hard-docked," he heard the mate say, an instant after he felt the bump.

"Jolly good," said the captain. He clicked the intercom. "All hands, stand down from stations. We're in Dylstra docks. Four-hour liberty—starting now." He clicked off the intercom.

Mike breathed a sigh of relief and turned to leave the bridge.

"Mike. Not you. I need you here for the unloading. I want to show you how it works." The captain grinned at Mike's expression of disappointment. "Don't worry—you aren't old enough to go into the saloons yet, anyway. You'll have plenty of time for that nonsense when you're a little older. Right now, you have more important things to think about—like learning the business."

Mike swallowed. "Yes, sir." It was happening exactly as Mary-All and Craig had predicted.

"Have a seat and I'll be with you in a minute."

Mike cleared his throat and said, "Uh, if it's all right, Cap'n, there was something Mary-All needed me for, before she goes on her liberty. She said to come down after shutdown. I don't think it'll take but a few moments."

"Eh?" The captain had already turned away to do a log entry. He looked up. "Mary-All? What for?"

Mike shrugged, and thought quickly. "It's, uh—I think, an adjustment to the fusion modulator. She wanted to make sure it was—"

"All right." The captain waved him out. "Be back in ten minutes, no more."

"Yessir."

A minute later, Mike was on his way down the central passageway to the engine deck. Dixie met him at the door, handed him a small duffel bag, and pointed toward the far end of the compartment, where Mary-All had a hatch open. Mike looked questioningly at the bag. "It's from us," Dixie said. "It's got your clothes in it. Now get going." She socked Mike on the arm. "And good luck."

Mike clutched the bag and headed for the open hatchway, which he knew led to the maintenance crawl-space surrounding the fusion engines. "Thanks," he murmured.

"You understand, now?" Mary-All said. "You'll wait by the emergency exit hatch until I open the lock from here. I'll do that as soon as Dixie tells me the captain's away from his monitors. I'll give you twenty seconds to get out before I close it again." She grinned. "There isn't enough radiation in there to hurt you—as long as you aren't in there more than a few minutes." She winked.

Mike nodded and tried to think of something to say, some way to say good-bye. "Are you sure you—that you won't be in any—"

Mary-All pushed him through the hatch. *"Go."* As he turned one last time, he saw a bright grin cracking her dark face again. "And win a race for us, okay?"

Mike grinned back. Then Mary-All slammed the hatch, and he began climbing through the cramped space separating the quark-plasma thrust tubes from the outer hull, and wondered uneasily how long "a few minutes" really was. In his head he ran through the calculations of residual radiation and exposures, but he'd never studied this stuff properly. He wasn't so sure that his escape wouldn't leave him with a radioactive glow.

Dixie waited in the passageway near the bridge until she heard Mary-All on the intercom, saying, "Cap'n Ess, this is engine deck. Is Mike being held hostage on the bridge? I need him here." Dixie held her breath, waiting for a reply.

When it came, it was in the form of the captain barking back over the intercom, "Mike Murray, report! Engine deck, he left here the minute we docked. Mike, report at once! Where in blazes are you?"

There was a period of silence, and then the captain

thundered out of the bridge, his bulk filling the passageway. "Have you seen Mike?" he bellowed at Dixie as he loomed toward her.

"Sorry, skipper. Don't know. I was just on my way off to see about getting provisions ashore—"

The captain passed her with a snarl, practically flattening her against the wall. He disappeared down the passageway, growling, "When I find that boy, I'm going to teach him the meaning of orders . . ."

Dixie took a breath, then slipped onto the bridge, peeking first to make sure no one was still there. She scanned the outside security monitors to verify that the coast was clear, and clicked the intercom to engine deck. "Mary-All, Dixie. All ashore that's going ashore." She clicked the intercom off, smiled to herself, and sauntered toward the exit portal.

Mary-All breathed a sigh of relief when she heard the call from Dixie. She hadn't wanted to say so, but she really hadn't been sure that the ruse would work. But it was no good standing here congratulating herself. With a quick lookout glance for the captain, she hit the switch to open the outer access hatch.

Godspeed, Mike Murray, she thought as she counted slowly to twenty.

Time seemed to have come to a standstill where Mike was, wedged between a bracing crossmember and the outer hatch. He could only wonder what was happening beyond the inner bulkhead as he imagined radiation emanating from every inch of wall surrounding him. There's not that much radiation, he told himself hopefully. But every vibration he felt could be the captain, coming to haul him out. And what was the penalty for mutiny, on a smuggling ship? How fast could he go from being the skipper's favorite to being ejected from an airlock as an example to others? And what of his friends? Mary-All had sworn they were in no danger, but he knew the captain wouldn't go easy on them if—

The hatch opened with a hiss.

Mike pulled himself into the opening and peered out, unbelieving. He was some distance above the hangar floor; but he was also weightless, and there was nothing to stop him from leaping straight across to the hangar exit. Was that someone waving at him from across the way? *Of course, idiot—it's Craig, and if you don't get moving, this hatch is going to slam and you'll be hamburger.*

Taking a deep breath, planting his feet, gripping his duffel, he leaped out into open space and sailed . . .

. . . and had enough time to hope no one except Craig was watching him . . . and to realize that he was sailing wide of his aim, he was going to miss the exit, he was going to *crash into the window of the control office if he didn't do something.* But there was nothing to grab, no way to deflect his flight path, unless . . .

With a gulp, he hoisted his duffel bag over his head and hurled it as hard as he could toward the hangar floor, in the direction of Craig. The reaction-thrust was small, and it set him tumbling, but was it enough to alter his trajectory away from the window? He held his breath and extended his arms and legs to slow his tumbling, and he glimpsed the wall coming up—*he was going to miss the window*—and then he hit, colliding with the wall and rebounding slowly . . . and his shoulder throbbed from the impact, but he managed to snake out a hand and grab a railing to stop his movement.

Pausing for breath, he reoriented himself, and saw Craig darting out to capture his duffel bag for him and then gesturing urgently. Mike nodded and waved back—but then froze when he looked back up at the ship and saw Bowker Ferguson moving about on the outside of the hull, making a maintenance inspection. The first mate seemed not to have seen Mike. If he did, would he blow the whistle?

Mike didn't dare take the chance of attracting attention. He crouched to make himself small and waited until Fergie had passed around to the other side of the ship. Finally Mike hurled himself toward the exit. This time his aim was better.

The captain was livid, but Mary-All simply shrugged and said, "Skipper, he didn't show for his duty. What can I tell you?"

"You'll tell me if you know where he went!" the captain snarled. "If that boy jumped ship, I'll kill him." He paused, fuming. "And that goes for anyone who helped him. Do you know what it's like to try to find talent like that in a kid? And this one just walks into my hands?"

"Well, skipper, looks like mebbe he just walked out of your hands," Mary-All drawled. He glared at her, and she said, with a shrug, "Why, Captain, you weren't thinking of *shanghaiing* the boy, were you? You knew he had other ideas what he wanted to do with his life."

The captain's glare deepened with suspicion. But Mary-All was confident that he wouldn't make an accusation. He needed his crew as much as they needed him, and there was a fine line between asserting his authority and abusing it. He's mad, but he'll get over it, she thought.

He grunted finally and turned away, growling, "My own crew! I'll be bejoogered. . . ."

Craig got him through customs with a carefully averted glance from an official on duty, then they hurried off toward another part of the docks. Mike was soon lost, and grateful that at least Craig seemed to know where he was going. But Craig wasn't saying anything, and wouldn't answer any questions—not until they reached a place in the entertainment sector called Stim's City, at first glance a bar. On second glance, many of the patrons were wearing temple electrodes as well as sipping from variously colored vials. Many of them were humming, laughing, moaning; it was a weird choir of voices. Not all were humans; there were several tall, blue-skinned Poldavians among them, heads bowed, lost in whatever it was they were receiving from the electrodes. Mike blinked. He wasn't used to seeing aliens in the flesh. What *were* they feeling from those electrodes anyway? Mike knew nothing of Poldavians, really; but he warily imagined them bursting free of their headsets and rampaging wild-eyed through the corridors.

The doorman waved Craig toward a back room, after glancing curiously at Mike. Craig's expression was uncharacteristically dour as they passed through the bar. "What *is* this?" Mike murmured. His friend didn't answer. "Craig?" he persisted.

Craig stopped at the door to the back room. He turned, gazing around as though seeing the room for the first time. "Pleasure-center brain-stim," he said.

Mike caught the disapproving tone. He looked at Craig questioningly.

Craig shrugged. "Nothing wrong with it, I guess. Except, you see those guys over there?" He pointed past a bank of colored lights to a pair of shockingly haggard men with wires attached to their heads. Their eyes were wide—too wide. "In any place like this, you'll see guys like that. Probably been here for days. They can't have more than an hour at a time, but there's nothing to keep them from coming back, and back. I've seen men squander entire fortunes in places like this, and when they're done, when they walk out, they've got . . . nothing."

Mike swallowed. "Not even memories?"

Craig looked at him sharply. "Yeah, I guess they have memories. But the memories just make them want more." Craig turned and palmed open the door.

Mike pressed his lips together and followed him through.

The back room was brighter. A man with a dark beard was yelling on a phone, and someone else in the next room was singing to himself in an excruciatingly out-of-key voice. After a few moments, the first man stopped yelling, and signed off and turned. He jumped to his feet. "Craig Show, you old swamp lizard! How are you?"

"Fine. Just fine," Craig said. "Look, this is the young fellow I was telling you about—Mike Murray, meet Davvid Andresun. Mike's in a bit of a jam," he said as the two shook hands. "I was hoping you might be able to help."

Davvid looked Mike up and down. "Sure, what do you need? False ID? Papers? Cosmetic surgery?"

"No, no," Craig said, chuckling as Mike drew back. "I'm just looking for someone to hook him up with. Someone who might be able to help him get to Clypsis." He explained, briefly, Mike's predicament.

Davvid cackled with laughter. "Bent tried to shanghai him? That old crook! Hoo boy, is he going to be sore when he finds out—"

"Yeah, yeah," Craig said. "He'll live. Look, I'm kind of tight for time. Do you think you can do anything?"

Davvid scratched his beard. "Well, I might. Clypsis, huh?" He scratched his neck. He leaned back in his chair and shouted into the next room. "Hey, Dennis—you know if Jass Blando's still in the system? Has he left for Clypsis?"

The singer burst into a pure operatic tenor—then stopped. "Blando? I don't think so."

"Don't think so, *which*?" Davvid shouted. "Has he left or not?"

"I saw him the other day. He was staying—"

"Right—I know." Davvid snapped on his phone and began punching a number. He glanced up and paused. "You know him?"

Craig coughed and glanced at Mike. "We were shipmates once."

"Great! Small world! He ought to be happy to do you a favor, then!" Davvid continued punching the number.

"Yeah—he ought to," Craig murmured. He sighed. "Except . . ."

Davvid completed the call and asked for Blando. He looked up. "Except?"

"Well . . ." Craig cleared his throat noisily. "Actually, he was a little mad the last time I saw him. I, uh . . . I owe him money." Craig's voice dropped. "A *lot* of money."

CHAPTER 5

Jass Blando was a man in his late thirties, of medium build, with short gray hair and bright blue eyes. He was whistling as he walked into the room; then he saw Craig. "You!" he shouted. "I never thought *you'd* have the nerve to let me see your face again, much less come crawling for a favor! What is it you want from me?"

Mike saw Craig's face grow pale. Blando strode angrily across the room and cocked his fists. Craig stood his ground, but kept his hands at his sides. Blando snarled and swung—and with a great cry, changed his motion in midswing and thumped Craig soundly on both shoulders. "You old possum! How the hell *are* you, anyway?"

The color slowly returned to Craig's face as it became clear that Blando's apparent rage had turned to laughter. Craig replied, in a voice that started as an astonished murmur and ended in a roar, "I'm fine . . . and what's the idea of barging in here like that? *Don't you know you could give someone a heart attack?*"

Blando guffawed and stepped back. "Well, you owed me, buddy—you owed me!"

Now Craig's face turned red. "I know I owed you. I still owe you. And I can't pay you." He hesitated a moment. "Well, I guess I could pay you a little bit. . . ."

Blando shook his head. "Debt's forgiven, pal. A long time ago." He shrugged, and added amiably, "I guess I have an unpaid debt or two myself. So, what brings you to this fair corner of the galaxy? And how is that fat old thief Bent?''

With a laugh, Craig said, "Well, he's not any thinner. He's still up to the same tricks."

Blando nodded and looked at Mike. "And is this one of your new recruits?"

"Well, in a manner of speaking. Josiah had figured on recruiting him for a little longer than Mike figured on serving." Craig introduced Mike and explained his situation. "I was looking for some way to help Mike get to Clypsis, and I thought of Davvid, who as you know has more fingers than an Argylian octopus, and he, being as always ready to help, came up with you." He shook his head at Davvid Andresun, who'd been watching in silent amusement. "So, Jass, what's taking *you* to Clypsis? Don't tell me you've given up pirating..."

Jass looked scandalized. "Please! Never have I pirated! Smuggling and pirating are very different skills, as you of all people should know!" He grinned slyly. "Anyway, I've gone back into racing, old buddy."

"What?"

"Don't sound so surprised. I used to talk about it all the time."

"You *talked*, sure! But you mean you really did it? You're racing again?"

Jass nodded. "Got a ship waiting for me now. I'm not getting rich, mind you." He laughed. "I still have to do some old-fashioned shipping between races, to keep body and soul together. But I have hopes."

"So don't we all," Craig murmured. "So don't we all." He glanced at Mike and grinned. "I hope you're properly impressed. You've now met your first official representative of the Clypsis racing establishment."

Mike nodded silently. As a matter of fact, he *was* impressed. Speechless, actually.

"The thing is," Craig continued, "I have to get back to the *Queen* before Bent takes off without me. What do you say, Jass? Can you help us out? If not, I'll have to leave Mike to his own devices."

"Just a ride to Clypsis?" Jass asked. "No problem. In fact, your timing is astonishing even for you, Craig. I'm leaving this evening; straight shot to Clypsis in three days. That okay with you, Mike?"

Blinking, Mike nodded and managed to stammer his thanks. "I'm—I mean, ready—this is all I have," he said, hefting his duffel bag.

"Good enough." Jass raised his eyebrows and stuck his hand out to his former shipmate. "Well, old partner—good to see you again. Even if you are still shipping with that scoundrel. Give my best to the old fool, and to Vicky Slicky, if she's still with you."

"She is, and I will," Craig said. "As soon as things get back to normal, that is," he added, with a wink at Mike. "Take care, you two. Listen to what this guy tells you, Mike. He's got a lot of valuable experience."

"I will," Mike promised.

"Don't *believe* him. But listen to him." Mike grinned. Craig shook hands and tossed a salute to Davvid. Then he turned and was gone.

Jass's ship, *Nighthawk,* streaked away from Dylstra at a speed that would have left *Swamp Queen* standing still, had the two been racing. *Nighthawk* was a small, sleek ship with oversized fusion drives—a solo-rigged ship with state-of-the-art astronics. Jass assured Mike that it was pretty stodgy compared to the racers he'd be seeing soon. "She was once a smuggler," Jass admitted. "Her owner used to hire a guy who's now a prize-winning racer to fly her on fast runs into some of the newer settlements, where the patrols are a little sparse. Not like your old boss, Josiah, who uses wiles rather than speed to get his cargo past the authorities. Now I'm flying her with perishable pharmaceuticals, which is *sort* of what the other guy was carrying—except that we're legal now and the drugs are on the up-and-up. You want to run this calculation for me?"

Mike agreed, and under Jass's watchful eye, he computed the entry angle for their shiftover into subspace. When Jass had approved his results, he said, "What was it, Jass?—between you and Craig. Are you good friends? He looked like he was expecting you to hate him. Did he really owe you a lot of money?"

For a minute, Jass didn't answer him. Mike turned and saw Jass looking thoughtfully at him, a tiny smile playing about the corner of his mouth. "Sorry," Mike said, thinking he'd overstepped his bounds. "I don't mean to pry."

. Jass shook his head, still smiling. "No, Mike—I was just thinking. Thinking about how mad I was at him... Yeah, we split, and he owed me a lot, and he didn't have it, even though I knew he *had* had it. I was fit to be tied, all right." He paused to do a position check, then continued, "The thing about Show, you see, is that he's always cared about doing the right thing for the other guy. Even if it costs him. Except on that occasion, I didn't happen to be the other guy." Jass laughed. "Don't get me wrong. He's no saint. But at least he cares."

"But—" Mike was confused. "Why did he—?"

"Ah. I didn't find out until half a year later. *Half a year I was mad at him.*"

"But what did he do with the money?"

Jass chuckled. "He used it to get a guy out of trouble. A racer, I found out later. A guy who'd gotten into hock, and had stupidly gotten mixed up in something real dumb—who was at his wits' end and about to do something even dumber, something *real* bad, except Craig heard about it and bailed him out with his own money." Jass shook his head admiringly.

"And yours?"

"And mine. Right. Except he didn't *tell* me what he'd done, and I only found out by accident later. I think he was afraid I wouldn't have thought this guy worth bailing out, or something. I don't know."

Mike considered that. "Would you have? Considered him worth bailing out, I mean?"

Jass smiled. "*Touché*. I don't know, to tell you the truth. He was an ex-smuggler like us—a brother of the spaceways—but you know, I never really thought that

57

much of most smugglers. I guess I liked to think that I was just an exception." He shook his head again, this time without admiration.

Mike ran his fingers through his hair thoughtfully. "Hm. Is it true, then, that a lot of racers got started in the smuggling business?"

"Oh, yeah, sure," Jass said. "Absolutely. Some guys because they love the thrill. Some—like me, and, I guess, you too—because it was the only way they could see to get out of whatever hole they were in and make their way to Clypsis. I never liked it, myself—though I have to admit I sometimes got a charge out of the actual runs."

Mike thought about Yolaan's World . . . the adrenaline rush as he'd struggled to save his shipmates from exposure . . . and later, his second thoughts. He wondered if that was how Jass had felt.

"Anyhow," Jass continued, "one thing you'll learn real fast about the racing world is that there are all kinds of people. Some you can trust like your brother, and others you won't even want to turn your back on. It's not always easy to tell which is which."

"You mean racers?"

"I mean racers, backers, managers, mechanics, pitworkers, bettors . . ." He glanced at Mike and chuckled. "Well, it'll be an education. You'll just have to learn to watch your step."

Mike considered his remarks in silence. Clypsis and Pitfall were places known to him only through the holos, and he kept trying to put Jass's comments into the mental picture of the place that he already had. Jass had already tried to discourage him from any expectations of easy opportunity in the racing world. *More people go broke without even entering a heat than ever get a chance to race for real,* he'd said. Well, statistics didn't impress Mike that much. He wasn't going all this way just to go broke.

"What's it like?" he asked, after a while. Jass had just finished the final course adjustments, and they had a few minutes left before subspace.

"What's what like?"

"The racing. I know what it looks like. What's it *feel* like?"

Jass smiled. "Ah. That."

"Yeah! That!"

"Well, I'll tell you. It's hard to describe." Jass thought about it for a minute. "There's nothing else like it, really. It's like riding a chute at five times the speed of light, and knowing that it wouldn't take much to put you over the high side of lightspeed for good—if you know what I mean."

Mike grunted that he thought he did.

"Of course, you know that the *entire system* is the racecourse. It's something to see, all right." Jass cocked his head wistfully for a moment, and seemed about to say something—but then it was time for the shiftover into subspace.

For three days, Mike peppered Jass with questions. Questions about the system, about racing, about life as an aspiring racer, about everything else he could think to ask. He felt thoroughly at ease with Jass, and it was obvious that there was a lot the older pilot could teach him. Besides, he thought—not without a touch of cynicism, since he seemed always to be saying good-bye to his friends—he probably ought to make the most of this time with Jass. Maybe this time it would be different, though; at least he and Jass were bound for the same place.

For his part, Jass seemed happy to talk to Mike about racing and Clypsis, but he also wanted to know what preparations Mike had made for his new, hoped-for career. "I can see you've spent some time on computers," he said, by way of complimenting Mike on his navigational skills.

"Quite a bit," Mike said. "Your system here is easy, compared with what Vicky made me go through on the *Swamp Queen*." In fact, the advanced astronics on *Nighthawk* made child's play of subspace entry calculations, compared to the complex setup required on Captain Bent's decrepit old freighter.

"Well, be glad she taught you that stuff," Jass said. "You might not need it right now, but someday it'll stand you in good stead. What else have you studied?"

Mike tried not to sound boastful. "I've got three certificates for computerized simulation training. I've taken the complete general space pilot's course on my homeset, plus some fusion engineering and navigation."

Jass's eyebrows went up. "All that? And you aren't even old enough to be out of school yet?"

Mike shrugged. "Been doing it as many hours a day as I could, for as long as I can remember."

"Mm." Jass nodded and got up to make a pot of Rigellian coffee. When he returned, he handed Mike a steaming mug and sat down with one of his own. Directly over his head was a small engraved sign warning against eating or drinking at the console. Jass saw Mike noticing it, and he chuckled. "Ah, hell," he said finally. Mike peered at him inquisitively. "Maybe you'll make it, after all," Jass muttered. "Maybe you will."

Mike didn't answer, but he sat back in his seat and sipped the thick, sweet coffee, and allowed a smile to cross his face.

Their first glimpse of the racing system came immediately after their shift out of subspace. *Nighthawk* rotated smoothly, and the viewscreen filled with a breathtaking image of Clypsis and her family. At the center of the system was the star itself, a blazing yellow sun, encircled by half a dozen planets of varying size and color. *Nighthawk* was approaching from well above the plane of the ecliptic, so that virtually the entire system was visible.

There was one dramatic feature of Clypsis itself—an enormous tail on the sun, a streamer of fiery plasma that arced up from its surface in a great twisting strand and coiled into a tight spiral in space, ending in a tiny glowing ring near the sun. That, Mike knew, was the curious phenomenon dubbed the Dragon's Claw: literally a fountain of starstuff being pulled into a diamond-like structure at the center of that ring—at the tip of the "claw"—as it circled close to the outermost layer of the sun. The "diamond" was a sphere of tightly warped space, an alien field effect producing a *hollow sphere* only a couple of dozen kilometers across. In the center of that sphere, he knew, was the inhabited racing complex known as Pitfall.

"There's a race under way," Jass remarked.

Mike was still trying to catch his breath. "How can you tell?"

"See the speedway web—at right angles to the ecliptic, in the plane of Pitfall? Wait—let me fix the polarization . . ." Jass made an adjustment on the console and the sun darkened, while another structure, which had barely been visible before, brightened. It looked like an enormous luminous spiderweb, surrounding the sun. It was the racing warpweb: a vast, intricate system of tubelike channels of highly stressed space, through which racing ships zoomed at multiples of lightspeed.

"That's it!" Mike yelled. He thumped the console and turned to Jass with a grin.

Jass grinned back. "Yup."

"Well, *hell's bells!"* Mike howled. He'd been waiting so long for this, the elation simply exploded in him. He thumped the console again and took a closer look.

Like fine luminous threads of spider's silk, the racing web encircled the sun in roughly concentric patterns. The array was mostly in a single plane that stood perpendicular to the ecliptic, the plane of the planetary system. The two planes intersected, passing through one another, the speedway web looking almost like a ghostly, radioactive shadow of the planets' orbits and the commercial warp-tubes that connected them. As Jass fiddled with the viewscreen controls, Mike began to see the finer structure of the warpweb—the circular courses, as well as others that were elliptical, and some distorted, kinked loops.

"Look in the third ring out from the sun. See those bright spots moving through the ring?"

Mike looked. Clustered on one side, following one

another along the ring, close together, were a half-dozen variously colored flecks of light, like tiny droplets of glowing liquid, streaming along the web. "Racers," Mike murmured happily.

"Yep. I'd say, at a guess, that they're doing about transfactor four—that's four times lightspeed."

"Yeah? Are they—?"

"Whups—check out ring five—another race just started." Jass pointed, and then Mike saw a tightly bunched cluster of droplets moving in the larger ring. "They just came out of the spin-up circle. You'll see them spreading apart a little as they jockey for position," Jass said. "The lead ship will settle into the groove—the fastest part of the racing tube—there, you see, one's pulling away now."

Mike watched for a few moments without speaking. It was an eerie sensation, to watch a race *around a sun,* from a distance that made it all seem as though they were watching miniatures on a table.

"Of course, we're a little behind in what we're seeing," Jass added with a chuckle. "We're still—let's see—about a light-hour out from the sun, so we're seeing what happened an hour ago. That inner race might even be finished by now."

"It's amazing that we can see them at all, from this distance."

"We're not actually seeing the ships, of course. We're seeing a radiant effect of their fusion drives passing through the warp field."

Mike nodded. Almost all of the racing took place at faster-than-light speeds, in the web system created by the same ancient alien technology that was responsible for the existence of Pitfall. He'd studied the profiles until he could recite them in his sleep. Clypsis was the only solar system in the known galaxy devoted entirely to the pursuit of racing. No one came here who wasn't interested in racing, and just about anyone who loved racing would beg, borrow, or steal to get here. It was hard to believe, even as he gazed at the system with his own eyes, that he had made it.

"What's that?" he asked, pointing to the outer edge of the web system. There were a number of discontinuous strands, some of them oddly curved, like threads from a fraying fabric.

"Ah," Jass said. "That's the new course they've been working on. It's for rally-style racing, in and out of the web, with all kinds of beacons and targets for the racers to pass in the sublight part of the race. We've already got that on a small scale—look at ring seven—it's discontinuous, too, but it's a lot more regular than the new one." He paused. "Those will be the proving grounds for the very top racers. It's tougher, and a lot more dangerous. You come out of that web at lightspeed or over, and *fffffftttt* . . . that's all she wrote."

Mike nodded. Danger was a part of the life here; it only made sense that some courses were more dangerous than others. "I'd like to try that sometime," he murmured, more to himself than to Jass.

Jass glanced at him with a chuckle. "Would you? Well, we've got something else to do first."

"What's that?"

"We've got to make entry into Pitfall. You're about to take your first ride through the web."

Mike looked blank, until Jass switched the view to another angle. Ahead of the *Nighthawk* was a glowing halo of light. "Ah," he said.

"You understand?"

"Well, the only way into Pitfall is through the warpweb. We can't go through the racecourse, so . . ."

"So they've got entryways spotted throughout the system, for incoming ships. Right." Jass was now turning his attention to the controls, performing rapid navigational operations. He made a small correction. "Okay. We're on the beam."

The halo was growing larger. Mike watched it, scratching his head. "Why don't we see the tube leading to Pitfall?"

"Funny thing about that," Jass said absently. "The closer you get, after a certain point, the more diffuse they look. The other thing is that these aren't racing tubes. They're slower, wider, less dense, more forgiving. So the energy fields are softer. They don't soak up so much radiation to reradiate. Five seconds . . . four . . . three . . ."

Mike took a breath and sat back.

The halo dissolved into a haze of sparkles; then the black of space disappeared and they were arrowing through an alien tube of shimmering light toward a tiny, distant point of darkness.

CHAPTER 6

The darkness leaped up to swallow them, and Pitfall sprang into view like gold at the end of the rainbow. The first thing that caught the eye was the mini-sun at the center of the darkness, a blazing jewel surrounded by a crazy-quilt ring structure which only slowly, as *Nighthawk* approached, resolved into an enormous complex of docks, hangars, and habitations: Pitfall. Etching a pattern around them in the darkness were stars, regularly spaced, which Mike soon realized were markers on the inner wall of the warp sphere that now enclosed them.

Jass tended to the flying, leaving Mike to puzzle out the view for himself. They had emerged from the warptube at the modest velocity of twenty meters per second, and at this point they were free to maneuver within the traffic patterns to the complex in the center of the sphere. He noticed a formation of ships expanding outward from the central structure toward the equatorial wall. "Race getting started," Jass observed. "Heavy racing day today. There's a kilometer-wide band all around the equator that provides entry to the web system. First they go to the spin-up ring for positioning and acceleration, then straight into the raceway proper."

Jass pointed ahead. "They come back through the north pole. All outside traffic, like us, comes in from the south." Jass began adjusting his instrumentation. "Let me find our docking beacon here. There it is. Purple light, near the right-hand edge of the ring."

Mike held the rest of his questions and let Jass work as they closed with the central structure. It was a more complex conglomeration than it had appeared from a distance. On the outside, and most prominent, was the main docking ring, encrusted with hangars and ships and repair bays, and flickering with arc lights and coded beacons. Nested inside the main ring, at various angles, were half a dozen other rings, holding (he assumed) the habitation areas and everything else—in short, the racing town.

As they approached, he saw row upon row of racing docks and hangars, with just enough ships visible on the outside to tantalize him. Here were a couple of class-three grand-prix-style racers, and there were a cluster of tiny A-class apprentice-stock racers. His heart thumped as a massive Five Star Special idled out of its dock. What famous figure, he wondered, was flying that one?

The racers and the racing docks passed behind them as they circled the Pitfall complex. Jass maneuvered smoothly toward the freight area—equally busy, but with hulking cargo carriers and slim couriers, and other familiar traffic such as Mike had seen at ordinary orbital stations. An empty dock bracketed by winking lights loomed dark before them, and Jass brought *Nighthawk* gently into her assigned berth. Powering down, he sat back and made his log entry. *Arrival Pitfall, 1324 hours*. He glanced up and smiled. "Another safe delivery."

Mike nodded, but felt a constriction in his throat. "Hey, hey," he said. "Uh, where do we go now? I need to find a place to stay, I guess."

"Time enough for that later. You want to hang around while I sign *Nighthawk* back to her owners? If you want, then, you can come with me to the racing pits and meet my crew and see the ship."

"Are you kidding!"

"Sit tight then. I'll be right back." Jass disappeared out the exit. Mike gnawed a Georgia maca-nut while he waited. Twenty minutes later, Jass came back and hooked a thumb toward the hatch.

Pitfall, on the inside, conveyed a feeling of linearity; everything was strung out along the ring. The racing sector was a considerable distance around from the freight area. They took a free-fall tube, hanging onto a slender moving filament along with dozens of other people. They passed ten or fifteen step-off platforms, where passengers could cross over from artificial gravity to weightless motion. The tube was largely transparent, so they could see the docks as they passed. They couldn't get much more than partial glimpses of most of the ships, but Mike was fascinated nonetheless, mostly by the incredible variety—freighters and passenger ships at first, then racers.

Nor was his fascination confined to the docks outside. The variety of persons—and machines—riding the tube was just as great: maintenance and messenger robots of all shapes and sizes, humans of every description, blue-skinned and gray-skinned Poldavians, flinty-faced Rykells, Merkeks who looked as though they were perpetually sunburned, and others that Mike didn't recognize. Mostly there seemed to be oxygen- or modified oxygen-breathers in this sector. Those with different requirements tended to stay in their own areas, Jass said, though in the inner rings where the entertainment quarters were located, there was a more lively intermingling of species.

They got off the filament at ZZ-Gate, which, according to Jass, was where the best undiscovered racers stayed hidden while waiting to make their moves. He shot Mike a grin and said, "Too many of them stay undiscovered, because they never succeed in making their move." As they strode down the concourse to the docks, he added, "I don't expect us to be here much longer."

"Looks pretty good to me," Mike murmured.

The lineup of racing pits was mind-boggling. From where they stood, Mike could see just those racing ships that were in shirtsleeve maintenance areas, rather than in vacuum, and that was enough. He saw dozens of

A through AAA stock racers and some class one grands; he wondered where the really fast ships—especially the Five Star racers—were berthed. Everywhere, spindly-looking cranes were shifting and robot welders were sputtering. Where pit crews weren't working on spacecraft, they seemed to be working on the pits themselves, tearing down and rebuilding. It looked as though the entire dock structure was in a constant state of alteration. The workspaces all seemed littered with reactor components, derricks, cannibalized instrument consoles, and anything else that looked as though it could be of use, or might once have been.

"Down here," Jass said, turning into dock ZZ24, which was as cluttered as any of the others. He gestured with an open hand, and Mike stopped and lost his breath and stared. The ship in the midst of it all had a hazed silver-and-blue hull. It was a compact, nearly cylindrical cluster of engines and ramscoops; emblazoned on its side in black-and-gold letters was the name: *Silver Cannon*. Mike walked around the entire ship, drinking in the view. It took him a moment to locate the pilot's cabin, crammed onto the structure almost as an afterthought. The *Silver Cannon* wasn't quite like any design Mike had seen on the holos; but it was beautiful, and he said so. "I thought you might like it," Jass said, with a wink. "She can fly in anything from class-one to class-three races. Come on and meet the crew." He ducked under the base of the ship. "Yo, Andy."

A lanky blond-haired man with a ducktail haircut backed out of a gaping engine tube, followed by a monkey-sized robotic assistant, which squawked twice and then settled back on its haunches, eyes flickering. "Hey, Jass! When did you get back?"

"Just now. Andy, I'd like you to meet Mike Murray. Mike, this is Andy Veekle—we call him Andy the Vehicle." Jass chuckled as the two shook hands. "Andy's our chief tech and tube washer. And his right hand, Oso." The robot beeped. "Now, if Andy and Oso have done everything they were supposed to do while I was gone, this ship'll be ready to fly in three days. How about it, guys?''

''You expect to *fly* this thing?'' Andy asked incredulously.

Jass's eyebrows went up. He turned and nudged Mike. ''Don't worry about Andy, heh-heh. He's a great joker.'' He whirled. *''Aren't you?''*

Andy shrugged, grinning. ''Yeah, I guess I can get her to move by then. Don't worry, Jass.'' His boss snorted. ''Actually, we did run into some problems overhauling the magnetic intake,'' Andy said more seriously. ''But I think we can handle it. I'll start tuning the reactors by tomorrow night.''

''That's cutting it close,'' Jass said, his voice suddenly inflected with worry.

''What can I say? If we had the staff and equipment—''

''Yeah, I know,'' Jass said, cutting him off. ''You don't have to tell me how poor we are. I'm painfully aware of it already.''

Poor? Mike thought as the two launched into a technical discussion. It was astonishing—this ship must have cost millions; and yet, as he looked across at some of the other docks, he saw ships that looked newer, and he saw more heavy maintenance equipment, and he remembered Jass's comments about having to fly freighters between races.

When Jass finished his discussion with Andy, he showed Mike around the ship. Mike asked him about the financial difficulty. ''Well, we have some backing from a syndicate,'' Jass said. He pointed to the nose of the ship, where a flared structure was being worked on by another tech. ''That's the magnetic ramscoop. It funnels any dust or gas we encounter into the fusion reactor as raw—''

''I know,'' Mike said. He looked at Jass curiously. His friend seemed suddenly awkward.

''Ah, yeah—of course you do. Well, up there are the tracking sensors and the radiation-shield projectors.'' Jass frowned, pointing. "The syndicate provides the ship, but we have to put up the operating costs. That's why we have such a small crew, and we don't have a lot of the hot, new technology that the factory crews have. It's make or break for us. If we qualify for this race, we get more support. If we don't"—he glanced at Mike and suddenly grinned— "hey, that's what makes it a challenge, right? So. If you want to sign on and work with us, I can't pay much, but I can let you get your feet wet."

Mike's mouth dropped open. "You mean you want me to—"

"It's not permanent. But I think there's a spot open on my crew, and you've got some solid training. Are you interested?"

Mike could hardly answer. He didn't have to. Jass laughed and clapped him on the shoulder. "What do you say we find you a place to sleep?"

Mike finally found his voice. "You're on. Both counts."

"Well, then, let's go."

Before long, Mike was ensconced in a boarding house called Slezak's Sack-house. For a tenth of an I¥ a day, he had a cubicle just large enough to sleep and stretch out in. That was all he needed. He was rarely there; he practically lived in Jass's docking pit for the next three days. There was so much work to be done on the ship before the race, and Mike had so much to learn—far more than he'd *thought* he had to learn.

Most of the real maintenance was beyond his abilities at this point, notwithstanding the time he'd spent in programmed instructions back home. Andy and the others had years of experience knocking reactor engines apart and putting them back together, and there was just no way he was going to catch up in a few days, no matter how willing they were to show him tricks of the trade. Still, he spent plenty of time holding tools for the crew, punching numbers into the tracking computer for the tactician, sweeping the floor, and cleaning dirty tools.

On the day before the qualifying runs, Jass poked his head into the maintenance shed, where Mike was putting some electronic gear away. "Got an hour or two you could spare for a ride?" he asked Mike.

"Sure. You need me to pick something up for you?" Mike was beginning to learn his way around this section of Pitfall, and he was happy for any excuse to become more familiar with the place.

"No, I need someone to ride in the jump seat and keep an eye on some instruments for me while I take the *Cannon* out for a calibrating run. Everyone else is busy, and anyway, they've all been around the course before. Can I talk you into it?"

Mike tried to hide his grin. "What do you think?" He closed the electronics locker and followed Jass out to the ship.

The rest of the crew had closed all the access panels and pulled back their equipment. The outer door was open. Andy was just retracting the fueling probe; the tanks were loaded with deuterium-rich hydrogen, though as Jass remarked, on this run they'd be picking up most of their fusable fuel along the way with the ramscoop. They weren't going for any speed records this time around. As soon as Andy gave them a thumbs-up, they stepped across into weightlessness and boarded.

The cockpit was designed to seat two comfortably, if both were midgets. It took time for both of them to get settled and strapped in, without too many elbows in the eyes. Jass ran through a complete checklist even though Andy and the ground crew already had done so. It didn't matter *who* had done a checklist ahead of him, Jass explained cheerfully, or how many people; he always ran through it again himself. It was the best way he knew to stay alive in a risky occupation. While he did that, Mike spent the time familiarizing himself with the controls and instrumentation. He'd studied them before, several times— but this time it counted. He surveyed the displays calmly, marking in his mind where they were the same as in the sim trials he'd been through, and where they were different. By the time Jass had the systems powered up, Mike was ready.

"Andy, we're ready to exit," Jass murmured in his helmet.

"Shoving you out now," Mike heard Andy reply.

The craft rumbled—not with the power of her fusion unit, but with the vibration of the tractorized cradle. It took about a minute for the ship to make the twenty-meter journey to the outer vacuum dock, through the shimmering gray of the airscreen. Mike watched as the quicksilver gray covered the viewscreen like a film, then broke away to reveal the dark, stark structures of the outer docks. Jass was already talking to traffic control, clearing his departure path. His voice scarcely changed tone as he spoke to Mike, saying, "At five kilometers, we'll be running the drive fields up to full for ten seconds, no thrust. If everything reads clear, we taper back to idle on the main until we reach the spin-up ring."

"Roger," Mike said. The docks were already dwindling as Jass maneuvered with the smaller thrusters. A minute later, the whine of the drive rose through the cockpit—far louder than on any freighter—and Mike watched the instruments carefully. It felt good to him, and a glance at Jass confirmed his impression. The whine subsided.

They were approaching the inner wall of the sphere now, squarely on path to the equatorial band. Jass called for and received clearance to enter the spin-up section— and moments later the starlike beacons loomed close, then distorted and winked out, and the *Silver Cannon* shot into a shimmering whirlpool. The fusion drive roared, and the ship leaped from the whirlpool into a long, curving, iridescent tube.

"Transfactor one," Jass said. "One and a half . . . two . . ."

Mike puzzled over the instruments as the warpweb brought them up to multiples of the speed of light. It seemed as though they ought to feel something, but the

acceleration was mostly external to them; within the
warpweb, space itself was flowing at superluminal speeds,
and whatever acceleration the ship's drive provided was
relative to that flowing frame of reference. In the forward viewscreen, he saw streaming ghostlight, the walls
of the warptube becoming slowly transparent as they
reached a speed plateau of transfactor three. Through
the tube, he could see the greater part of the speedway
encircling Clypsis, the web loops pale gold against the
sun.

"What?" he said suddenly. Jass had spoken to him.

"Stay with it, Mike. What are the readings on magnetic stability?"

Mike hurriedly gave Jass the information he wanted.

"Good. Nice and smooth. You want to take it for a
minute while I check something out?"

Mike nearly choked. "Uh—sure." His hands settled
into the control recesses.

"Just keep her straight and center. No sweat."

Mike swallowed; he felt the control pass to his fingers
as Jass released it. For a few seconds, he scarcely breathed
as the ship flew at his behest, straight and true. Finally he
began to relax and to *feel* the control, the tiny adjustments
that were exactly like those he had made in simulators,
except that now the feedback was total. "Gonna kick her
up," he heard, and a moment later he felt a surge as Jass
shoved the drive up to full. There was a vibration he
wasn't sure he liked, but he focused on staying centered in
the tube and left the worrying to Jass.

"Okay, I've got her," Jass said a minute later, break-
ing into his dizzying concentration. Mike passed the control back to the older pilot and drew a deep breath.
"How'd it feel to you?" Jass asked.

Mike glanced at him and realized at once that the
question was technical, not personal. "I felt something
when you throttled up. Not sure what," he answered.

"Good," Jass said. "Well, not *good*. We had a
fluctuation in the magnetic containment. Andy'll have to
look at that when we get back." He glanced at Mike.

"Not everyone would have caught that on his first run."
Jass cut the throttle, made a few adjustments, then powered up again slowly. The vibration was gone. He repeated
the throttle-up, this time suddenly. The vibration was back.
Jass sighed. "All right. We've got a lot of other things to
go over. Bring up checklist Charlie on the screen and let's
get it done. . . ."

The flight was nearing its end before Mike had much
of a chance to look up again. When he did, it was to see
the great streamer of the Dragon's Claw arching over the
webtube ahead of them. They flashed under it a second
later, and then Jass was asking for more readings as they
veered into the pit lane for the return to docks.

Minutes later the light-spattered darkness of Pitfall
surrounded them again, and they approached the complex from the north pole at what seemed a crawl. Jass
brought the *Cannon* in to dock, and before they'd even
passed through the airscreen, Jass was on the com to
Andy. "I hope you weren't planning to get any sleep
tonight, because we've got a few more adjustments to
make . . ."

Race day. Mike was back at the pit extra early,
having barely slept a wink. He was the last of the crew to
arrive. He found Jass in constant motion around the ship,
talking in a soft voice with one crewman after another. He
nodded when he saw Mike and immediately put him to
work checking meters for Andy. Jass had scarcely left the
pit since the day before, it turned out, but somehow he
looked as rested and alert as ever.

Scant few hours remained before the start of the
qualifying trials, and Andy and Oso were still working to
correct the problem with the drive coils. "He can run
with it if he has to," Andy told Mike, "but we'd sure
rather he didn't. It'll affect his ability to accelerate for
passing—and it's the sort of thing that can go out under
stress."

"It won't blow, will it?"

Andy shrugged. "It shouldn't. But there are no guarantees in this business. Anyway, I think we've just about got it under control here. Keep watching that output . . .''

Jass walked by, scowling. The tension was rising steadily in the dock area. Mike had always known it would be high; on the home holocasts, the commentators always played it up, trying to generate their own tension, as well. But that was nothing like feeling it snapping in the air around you, penetrating your bones; it was something you could smell. And it wasn't just in Jass's dock, either. All along the row, crews were working to make ships ready, and the tension was thick in the air.

The public-address system came to life, calling the pilots to a final briefing before the start of the trials. Mike saw Jass heading down the concourse with the other competitors, and felt a twinge of envy. Don't complain, he told himself. Did you ever think you'd be standing in the Clypsis pit docks before your seventeenth birthday? It seemed no less than a miracle that he was here at all.

Andy closed up the diagnostics unit and called Oso out of the engine tube. The mech sidled out from under the ship. "You can go recharge, Oso," Andy said. "And that," he added to Mike, "is as close as we're going to get without putting in a new set of coils."

"It's too late to do that, I assume?" Mike asked.

Andy laughed. "We would have done it weeks ago, if we could have. But those babes cost, and Jass has already got everything he owns staked on this run. It's make—"

"Or break. I know," Mike said sourly.

"Yeah. Well, anyway, Jass'll want to roll out as soon as he gets back, so let's get things squared away here." Andy whistled to the rest of the crew, and everyone began pitching in to clear away the clutter.

Amazingly, after all the frantic activity leading up to this point, they now found themselves with time to kill, waiting for Jass to return. Mike went for coffee for the crew, and as he waited in line at the commissary, he surveyed the racing crowd. It was a varied crowd today—it seemed as though the start of a new round of racing brought all the elements of the racing culture out of their hiding places. The humans mostly appeared a rough-and-tumble lot, and the nonhumans hardly less so. There were a good many nonoxygen-breathers here, as well—wearing breathing tubes or helmets, or simply (it seemed) holding their breaths. After getting a whiff of a couple of them, Mike wanted to hold *his* breath.

Scanning the room, he looked up and saw a glassed-in balcony overlooking the floor. The people up there, from the glimpses he got, looked better dressed than those down below; and he thought he saw the flicker of screens and data boards. Bettors, he thought. So that's where they hang out. But, he realized, as he turned back to pay for the coffee, that was probably just where the lower-echelon bettors plied their trade. The wealthy syndicate bettors had their own ring, deeper in the maze that was Pitfall, complete with yachting docks and access to the headquarters of the Clypsis Racing Commission.

Returning to the dock, he found the crew gathered around Jass. Andy caught his eye and murmured, "Heat number three." He looked unhappy. Mike passed around the coffee and queried him with a glance. "Jass has never won a race with a three in it," Andy whispered.

Mike raised his eyebrows. "Oh." He thought a moment, then went to find his sweatshirt. In its pocket was his last bag of maca-nuts. He passed the bag around. "For luck," he said.

Jass held one of the giant glazed nuts up in salute. "For luck," he repeated. "Thanks, Mike."

It was time for rollout, and this time Mike watched from the dock as the *Silver Cannon* slipped through the shimmering gray airscreen to the vacuum dock. The crew operations changed to race status now: Mike stayed near the monitors where the racing telemetry would be coming in, transmitted through the warpweb at effectively faster-than-light speed. Andy and one other man suited up to station themselves at the outside dock; if Jass needed a quick-and-dirty repair, they'd be ready to handle it in vacuum, without taking time to bring the ship in.

Soon the announcement crackled: *"First qualifying heat for the Empire-Stars Class-Two Closed-Loop Championship now ready to begin. All crews signal readiness."* There was a short pause. Then: *"Pilots, test your engines."* A moment later: *"The yellow light is on. Pilots, move out to nine kilometers."* And finally: *"The spin-up circle is open. On the green light, the race begins."*

As Mike watched, a light on the console blazed green—and in the screens, he saw a dozen ships leap toward the equatorial band and vanish.

Ten minutes later, heat two began and the same scene was replayed.

Then heat three. Jass tested the *Silver Cannon*'s drive unit, and all the crew peered at the readouts for any sign of trouble. Clean and smooth, Andy announced. The yellow light came on, and Jass moved away from Pitfall. Voice chatter dropped to nil, as everyone awaited the signal. *"On the green light . . ."*

The console blazed green, and *Silver Cannon*'s drive blazed violet, and then Jass was gone, along with eleven other ships.

"Running a bit cool," came his voice. The images on the screen were scrambled for a moment, then they straightened out, and on the forward-looking monitor, Mike saw the shimmering walls of the webtube streaming toward him out of infinity, just as he had seen them yesterday—except that now Jass was jockeying for position against his competition. The spin-up ring was wider and slower than the actual raceway; there was enough room here to pass without too much trouble, but once they hit the raceway, that would no longer be true. Now was the time to capture the lead if he could.

"Where is he?" Mike whispered loudly.

He was answered by Jass's voice: "I seem to be fifth back. I'm going to make a jump for third." Several telemetry readings flickered as he pushed the drives to full.

"There it is again," someone muttered. "Fluctuation."

Two ships appeared in front of Jass's and appeared to

swerve aside as Jass maneuvered to pass. The image was obscured by glowing haze for an instant as the *Cannon*'s ramscoop greedily swallowed the exhaust of a competitor's fusion drive; then the *Cannon* glided past both ships. Ahead, two more ships were growing larger as Jass moved up behind them. "Getting some instability," Jass muttered, voice crackling. "I think I can ride it out."

"Don't push it too hard!" Andy warned.

"Yep." Jass sounded calm, almost bored.

Mike gripped the edge of the console. Jass was pulling up behind the number-two ship now. "How's my time running?" Jass asked.

"Borderline," the tactician answered. "I'd feel better if you were in the two position."

"Copy." Jass drew close to the second ship's exhaust. "I don't think this guy's going fast enough to let me trail him in."

It wasn't necessary to be number one, Mike knew—not for the heat. He just needed a fast enough time to qualify for the main race. But how fast was fast enough? There was no way to be sure.

Jass passed a series of marker lights, and the webtube walls contracted inward. He was out of spin-up into the main raceway now. "Damn," Jass muttered, trimming back to match speeds. The two ships ahead of him were in the groove now, the fastest part of the webtube. The only way to get by them was to pour on power and swing through a zone of turbulence into the passing lane.

Mike and the others watched in silence as the ships sped around the sun at four times the speed of light. The Pitfall racing monitor showed the ghostly web and the colored droplets of light streaming through it one after another. The violet one was Jass, close behind number two. The lead ship was drawing away.

"Jass, good buddy—the preliminaries don't look good," the tactician broke in. "Heats one and two are running fast. If you don't get around this clown, I've got a bad feeling."

"Keep that number-three coil damped down," Andy cautioned.

"Roger. Going for the pass now."

The telemetry signals jumped as Jass throttled to full power. He swung left to slip past his opponent.

"Jass, watch out for—!"

That was Andy, but Jass was already reporting, "I've got a leakage of plasma at the front pinch-ring. Losing power. Andy, can I bypass that to the second?"

"Try it, but first step down your condenser . . ."

In the monitor, it was clear for all of them to see. The number-two ship was pulling away. "Buggers." Jass was having trouble sliding back into the groove. There was a muffled curse, then Jass reported in a low voice, "That tears it; I've lost the ring. We're in a danger mode. Andy, I've got to come in."

Andy's voice sounded anguished. "Can you ride with it? You've only got half a minute to go."

"I know." Jass's voice was terrifyingly calm. "I know." He maneuvered the craft into the pit lane. "Gentlemen, we're out of this race."

It was a glum crew that met Jass as he stepped out of the *Silver Cannon*, but Andy was the first to extend a handshake, and the others followed suit quickly. Jass walked slowly around the base of the craft, studying it as though trying to understand how this could have happened. He didn't look like a man who was defeated, but it was clear that he felt this as a terrible blow. "Well," he murmured at last. "We knew we needed a number-three coil. Now we need a new ring, too."

He turned to gaze at his friends and laughed painfully. "I guess we need more than that now, too—don't we?" He looked back at the ship and sighed. "Well, gentlemen, I guess I don't need to tell you." His eyes met Mike's. "Sorry, Mike. I know I said that the position wouldn't be permanent. But I'd hoped it would last a little longer than this."

"You aren't . . . What? Are you *disbanding?*" Mike demanded in disbelief.

"That's the way of racing, my friend," Jass murmured, and the expressions on the crew's faces indicated that they already understood. Even the mechs looked somber. "It costs money that none of us have. Until we find new backing, the *Cannon* passes back to its owners. That means you and I—all of us—are out of a job together."

Mike gazed at him, at the others, stunned.

"It's the way of racing," Jass repeated with a shrug. "In together, and out together. It's just the way of racing. I'm sorry, Mike, I really am."

CHAPTER 7

Down and out on Pitfall.

Mike had a little money—enough to live on for a week or two, if he was exceedingly cautious. But Pitfall, he was soon informed, was unforgiving of indigence. The legal grace period for a new citizen without money or income was a week, and at the end of that time, any oxygen-breather failing to demonstrate a means of self-support was deported to the planet Enigma. (Where others were sent, he never learned.) On Enigma, the rumor went, one could find work to stay alive, but the cost to return was so high that many never made it back; they simply became permanent wage-earning citizens of Enigma.

That, Mike vowed, would happen to him over his dead body. But he had to find work, and fast. Jass could offer little help; he couldn't even pay his ground crew until he'd made another freight run for income. Mike was glad to waive his own minimal salary—it was a small sacrifice compared to everything Jass had already done for him—but it did mean that his own day of reckoning would come a little sooner. One thing Jass *could* give him was a good reference, and some advice. The advice was to take a day off to learn his way around, and then to look for work—*any* kind of work—not by going to the jobs clearinghouse, but by roaming the docks and asking.

He felt uneasy taking a day off when he knew his days were numbered; but he took Jass's advice anyway, and was glad he did. Not only did he finally learn the layout of the Pitfall rings, he also found a public-access library where he could pursue his studies for piloting and technical certification. He was tempted to sit down then and there with the computers, but reluctantly he decided to leave it for another day and continued his exploration of the inner rings.

Certain areas were off-limits to him, either for environmental reasons—like corrosive atmospheres, hypergravities, or steamy or freezing temperatures—or because only investors, bettors, and Racing Commission officials were permitted to enter. However, he strolled in a kind of nervous enchantment along ''the Strip,'' the recreation and entertainment sector. He'd never really had the freedom to peer at so many sleazy joints before, liquor and stim saloons, theaters of all sorts, cafes, and houses of legal prostitution.

Well. He had no money even if he'd had the nerve; and he recalled Craig Show's comments at the stim bar back on Dylstra. He did discover cafes offering ordinary food and drink, and even live entertainment, and he vowed that on the day he found employment, he would treat himself to a night out. Andy had talked to him about a couple of singers named Crystal Cashe and Alyson Avery, and when Mike came across their names on the front of a little den called The Wugbug, he made a mental note to return.

By the time he got back to ring two and his room at Slezak's Sack-house, he was feeling tired but a little less gloomy. There was hope, he felt now; all he needed was a good night's sleep. The morning, surely, would bring a job.

Morning might in fact bring a job, but it would not be the next morning. Mike got up early and traipsed the docks until his feet ached, and all he got for his troubles were a few polite rejections and many curt ones. By the morning of the third day, his spirits were sinking low again; and when he heard the words, ''Can you start today?'' he could hardly believe his ears.

An hour later he was on the ground crew of the XTP

factory team, led by a Five-Star class racer Mike knew by reputation: Dugg "Fast Rev" Stuart. Fast Rev was a big-leaguer, one of those careful, scientific racers known for steady performance and relentless perfectionism. Mike was stunned to find himself working for someone so well known; however, he soon learned that it was a large company, with a technical crew of over two dozen, plus seven pilots, and it wasn't clear when—if ever—he'd get to meet the Rev himself.

Still, it was work, and it paid, and that was what counted. If it consisted mainly of sweeping, scrubbing, emptying trash, and going for coffee, he wasn't going to complain. Just being around the docks, he got a good close look at three of the classiest racing ships he'd ever seen—a pair of beautiful two-drive bandits, and one gargantuan triple-drive long-hauler. Part of his job would be cleaning and polishing the ships' hulls, and that suited him just fine. The closer he got to the ships, the better he liked it.

His first day was so exhilarating, he hardly felt tired at quitting time. He was tempted to go spend the evening in the library, but he'd already made plans to meet Jass for dinner, and he remembered that he'd promised himself a night out to celebrate. He showered and changed, then headed for the inner rings.

He met Jass at the third-ring crossover, a clear-walled concourse from which one could look out past the intersecting rings and see the glint of the mini-sun in one direction, and in the other, ships moving to and from the web portals. Pitfall never slept, and there was scarcely a time when racers weren't moving through the webs, even if only in practice runs.

"Hey there, partner!" Jass called. "I hear you've moved up to the big time."

"I guess so," Mike said nonchalantly. "I get to *watch* the big fellows, anyway. I don't think I'll be riding around the track with any of them, though."

"Well, don't worry about that. You'll be getting good experience. Where do you want to eat?"

"Do you know a place called The Wugbug?" Mike asked.

"Andy's favorite place? Sure."

They made their way inward two more rings and some distance around, until they reached The Wugbug, which was in one of the sleazier sections of the Strip. He observed with satisfaction that the singers Andy had recommended were on tonight. He and Jass found seats near the front. They ordered sandwiches and turned to watch the show.

Crystal Cashe was the lead singer, a sexy brunette whose auburn-brown hair cascaded about her head and sparkled with a rosy glow whenever she reached deep for those long, heartrending highs. Her gown was so black that the eye couldn't focus on it; but as she moved about the stage, streaks of silver and gold flickered up and down her profile, to the whistles of an appreciative audience. Behind her, Alyson Avery sat amidst an array of electronic gear; she was an eyeful in a blazing crimson pantsuit that made her look like a living ruby fixed in a setting of black and chrome. She came in from time to time on harmony, but mostly she seemed to be in charge of the electronic wizardry that shimmered around Crystal's clear voice, augmenting and transmuting it and surrounding the two of them with ghostly holographic images:"... I'm going, gone, gone ..." Crystal sang.

Mike was so enchanted that he hardly noticed the arrival of their food. Jass poked him, and he started, then picked up his sandwich and munched in contentment as the two singers shifted into a new song: "... One word ... probably it will confuse ... but I guess it will have to do ... *Ngi ... ngi ... ngi ... ngikutzandza* ...." Mike had no idea what it meant, but he was dazzled by Crystal's voice and Alyson's second-beat harmony and the flow and dance of the visual effects.

The set ended, and Mike and Jass applauded and whistled with the rest of the crowd, then ate and talked about their respective plans for the future. Jass was going to be shipping out on a short freight run in a couple of days; he promised to let Mike know if anything came up that would be helpful. Mike, meanwhile, planned to learn as much as he could while moving up the ladder in his new racing crew.

Glancing up, he saw Crystal walking by on her way back to the stage. He made a silent gesture of applause, and Crystal grinned and stopped to say hello. "You're new here, aren't you?" she asked. "I don't think I've seen you before."

"I'm new to the whole system," Mike said.

"Well, we're glad to have new blood in the audience."

Mike smiled. "Can I ask you something?"

"Sure."

"In that last song . . ." Mike struggled to untie his tongue. "I couldn't quite . . . understand. I was just wondering—" he took a breath, trying not to show his self-consciousness, "what it meant."

"*Ngikutzandza?*" The singer beamed. "Thank you for asking! No one else here understands it, either—but they don't bother to ask."

Mike noticed Jass grinning, but he was determined to pursue the question. "Why, is it some—I don't know . . ."

She laughed. "You're from Earth, aren't you?"

"Why—yes. How can you tell?"

"Your clothes give you away. And the way you keep your hair." Crystal ruffled his unkempt hair teasingly. "Well, anyway, there's a place on Earth called Africa. Do you know it?"

Mike laughed. "You're the second person to ask me that! Is that the only place on Earth people know about?"

"Well, I don't know. I've never been there," Crystal said. "Anyway, I forget what language it is—some old dialect—but the word *ngikutzandza* means . . ." She paused and glanced at her approaching partner. "Alyson, tell him what *ngikutzandza* means."

"It means 'I love you,'" Alyson said. "In siSwati." She smiled brightly and continued on to the stage.

"Ah," Mike said, blushing deeply.

"We'll sing the next one for you," Crystal promised, and followed her partner.

Mike knew Jass was laughing deeply and quietly, but he refused to look at his friend's face. *I love you.* He ought to have known! Well, anyway . . . He turned with silent satisfaction to watch, as the two singers began their next set.

It was on his third day in Fast Rev Stuart's dock that he discovered a simulator in which, during off-hours, he could occasionally get in some practice. By this time, he'd already made himself familiar with the training programs available in the Pitfall library. The simulator would make a perfect complement to his evening studies.

Sleep? Who needed sleep?

His days soon consisted of a mélange of long work-days in the pits doing grunt work and little more, but at least being near the action, and better yet, being able to pause in his work once in a while to watch a run get under way. The competition for simulator time was stiff, and he was low man on the totem pole; nevertheless, he managed to squeeze in an hour from time to time. He picked up a few tips from some of the junior pilots, but for the most part he was on his own with the trainer and its computer.

He had a lot to learn, but he knew he was making progress. He was determined to work his way up the ladder to apprentice pilot, no matter how long it took. But there were so many people above him on the ladder!

So far, most of the racing activity had been in the A and AA classes, which were the minor leagues of racing, involving smaller ships and the more junior pilots, including apprentices. These, in fact, were the kinds of races that Mike hoped to get a shot at one day. Coming up soon, however, were the opening trials for a major Five-Star race, in which the Rev would be competing—the sort of contest that brought racing fever to a high pitch, not only in Pitfall, but out among the stars. For the first time, the senior pilot began appearing on a regular basis.

Mike knew that the racer was around, but he wasn't expecting to see him when he came out of the simulator late one evening, about two weeks after he'd come on. Stuart was at the computer console, looking thoughtful. He glanced up as Mike closed the door to the simulator chamber and registered out with his wristchip. "Mike Murray?" The pilot extended a handshake. "I haven't had a chance to say hello before. But welcome to the team."

"Thanks. I—didn't know anyone was here," Mike said, disconcerted.

"Oh, I don't always keep normal hours, but I'm around," Stuart said. "I was just doing some tactical modeling on the computer here. Big race coming up, and all that."

"I know," Mike croaked. "Was I—I mean, I'm sorry if I was taking time on the simulator—if—if you needed it."

"No, no. Actually, I was noticing your work in there. You have talent." The Rev smiled. "You aren't angling for my job, are you?"

"*No*—I mean—"

Stuart looked at him quizzically. "You're not? *Well, why not?* Everyone else is, around here—you should be, too! That's how you get ahead in this business!"

Mike groped to recover his voice. "Well—I'm studying . . ."

Stuart laughed, waving off his defense. "That's okay. I have enough competition already. Well, listen, keep up the good work."

"Thanks. I'm trying to spend as much time on the simulator as I can."

"I meant on the ground crew!"

Mike blinked, crestfallen. "Oh. But I thought you said—"

"That you have talent? Sure." The pilot's voice became more distant. "But you'll find it pretty hard to move up through the ranks of a big factory crew like this. Too many people older than you, all waiting in line. If you want a shot at apprenticeship, you'd better go off with one of the smaller teams. And if you do that, where will *we* be? Do you know how hard it is to find someone who cleans as conscientiously as you do?'' Stuart laughed, and there was a glint in his eyes that Mike couldn't interpret. ''Well, see you tomorrow.'' Stuart saluted and walked out of the docks.

Mike stared after him for a long time. Had he just been befriended by one of the great racers? Or snubbed? If snubbed, why hadn't the man come right out and told him to get lost? Stay a cleaner . . . a grunt? Never!

He sighed and shut down the simulator computer and headed back to his room, filled with troubled thoughts.

The following night the simulator was booked, so he went instead to the library. The place was quiet, nearly deserted, but he enjoyed it that way; he liked the feeling that the library was his private domain. He didn't mind sharing it with the human librarian—a short, cheerful little man by the name of Browser MacPhee—but he was happiest when he was the only one on the computers, which gave him the feeling that he had the full and undivided attention of the Brain Bank's library core. It was an illusion, of course, but what did he care? It was the feeling that counted.

After checking in with Browser, he found a carrel in one corner of the room and called up a program he'd already begun in warpweb engineering. As the holo diagrams rotated on the screen, he tried to stop thinking about the future of his career—would he always be going for coffee and sweeping floors?—and to focus instead on the complex theory and engineering that made this whole business possible. It was hard to concentrate, but the sooner he mastered this stuff the better. He'd already learned that when he had problems, he could go to MacPhee; Browser not only kept track of the library materials, he knew and understood most of it, too, and he was a racing enthusiast.

"Ought to be more young racers like you," the librarian had remarked once. "Too many guys think they can get the world on a string without learning the basics. But it doesn't work that way."

Mike shook his head, took a deep breath, and refocused his eyes. Gradually his thoughts meshed with the diagrams and text, and the program began to flow, and understanding to emerge.

It was during a short break, really no more than a fast stroll up and down the length of the library to get his blood moving, that he noticed the automaton. It was an energy-field robot: a silver-chrome base floating just above the floor, and projected up out of that base was a shimmering meter-tall column of translucent holographic light, enclosed by an energy field. It was gliding to and fro, as though looking for something. He peered at it curiously for a moment. This was no public-service robot; it must be a psyche-vehicle, an afterlife personality carrier for someone important. Someone rich, anyway. Mike sidled over to Browser's desk, and queried by tossing a glance in the automaton's direction.

"Speedball Raybo," Browser murmured with a nod. "See the rippling chevron pattern in his energy field? That's his ID mark."

Mike's eyes widened. "*The* Speedball Raybo?"

"There's only one. He went over the high side twenty years ago. But he'd had an imprint made just before the race, so we've still got him around, even if he's not incarnate."

Mike turned and gazed awestruck at the PV. So that was what remained of one of racing's greats? Many of Speedball's records had remained unbroken for years after the sudden end of his career—when his ship had emerged from a warpweb at greater-than-light speed and vanished in a spectacular blast of light and subatomic particles. That had happened before Mike was born; but Mike had watched replays of the great races a hundred times over, and he knew Speedball's stats as well as he knew anyone's.

He turned back to Browser. "Do you suppose I could—"

"You want to talk to him? Sure," Browser said. "Hey, Speedball, got a minute?"

The automaton turned and glided silently over to the desk. "What ho, Browser," it said, in a voice that sounded human yet had a faint overtone that was almost ...angelic?

"Looking for something?"

"Well, I was looking for some*one,* but he doesn't seem to be here." The silver base rotated, and the energy field sparkled, near eye level. "Who's your friend?"

Browser gestured. "His name's Mike. He's an up-and-coming young racer. Mike Murray, meet Speedball Raybo."

A slender graphite-composite arm emerged from Speedball's base, and a fragile-looking but undoubtedly powerful hand grasped Mike's in a firm handshake. "Pleased. I envy you," Speedball said.

"Huh?"

"Being a new and up-and-coming racer. I wish I could be in your shoes."

Mike's mouth opened, but it was a moment before anything came out. "But..." *Are you crazy?* he wanted to say. "You set more records than just about anyone who's ever raced here! I'd *love* to do a tenth that well! I haven't even raced yet," he babbled.

"Oh, well—I'm not complaining, mind you. And I am flattered," Speedball said, "that a young fellow like you knows his racing history well enough to know who I am, much less what my record is."

"Well, of course! You set the Five-Star record three times, and the original open-course record, and—" Mike paused for breath. "Well, it's not as if you don't know that stuff. But I could tell you just about everything you did, right up to the time that you—" Mike choked off his words. He'd almost mentioned the accident that had killed Raybo. Now, *that* was a good way to make friends!

The energy field that was Speedball flickered, and there was a sound of quiet laughter. "If you were about to talk about the time that I 'bought the sun,' don't worry about it. I don't remember it, you know. My imprint was made a week before. I just knows what I reads in the papers." Mike looked a little puzzled, and Speedball added, "I watched the replays, same as you. It was pretty spectacular the way I went out, wasn't it?"

Mike's mouth opened and closed. He glanced and saw MacPhee grinning. "Don't worry, Mike," Browser said. "He's had twenty years to get over it."

"That's right. So tell me, Mike, are you apprenticing with anyone?" Speedball turned as though to face Browser. "We have to look after our new racers, you know. Especially one who knows the important records in racing history!" He turned back to Mike, who by now was more than a little embarrassed. "What are you studying here?"

Mike told him, and explained that he was holding down a pit job for Dugg Stuart but didn't have an apprenticeship yet.

"Well, you keep at it," Speedball said. "I got started the same way. Sooner or later, something will come along that will spring you out. Fast Rev's a good man. But it's tough on those big teams. Get all the experience you can, but if you get a good chance to jump to a smaller team, I'd advise you to take it." The column of light swirled. "I must be going. Browser, thank you for your hospitality, as usual—and Mike, best of luck." The automaton glided away without another sound and left the library.

Mike gazed at Browser's grinning face in astonishment. "Wow," he said.

Browser nodded. "Wow, indeed."

Mike turned to go back to his computer studies, but he knew as he did so that it would be harder than ever to concentrate on theory now.

Speedball Raybo floated inward through the rings, toward the Racing Commission offices. He was headed for the Operations Committee, where he was scheduled to assist with monitoring on a series of qualifying trials for promising associate-class pilots. It was a duty that many of the older pilots, both incarnate and otherwise, considered tedious; but Raybo enjoyed it. He hadn't been kidding when he'd told the young Murray that he envied the youth's position and opportunity. The closest Raybo could come to starting a new career was to help young pilots get a fair chance wherever he could. At times he despaired, wondering if the crops of new young people would ever again be as good as they had been in his own day.

Today he had met a young man who could be an answer to that prayer. He wasn't leaping to any conclusions—he'd been disappointed before, too often to let his hopes rise far, or fast—but this one definitely bore watching.

Passing through the long, busy corridors of the Racing Commission, Raybo greeted dozens of people. Some he liked; some he didn't. He made it a point to be equally civil with all. It wasn't just that he liked people; indeed, many of them he heartily disliked and distrusted. But he had to work with them, and as a nonincarnate he at least had the advantage that his feelings were his alone, to display or conceal as he chose. And that could be important when he wanted to help a new prospect up through the minefield of racing's advancement system. It was easy for a novice pilot to find himself sponsored by the wrong person or the wrong syndicate. Too often Raybo had seen young careers manipulated and bled dry for the sake of someone's quick profit. A quiet assist at the right time could make all the difference.

To guide a beginner through this field *without* letting on his own involvement—that was the challenge that he most enjoyed.

Before entering the operations room, he stopped in the Commission Members' Lounge and found a secure phone connection. He had a report to make to an old friend of his—a Rykell nonincarnate who'd died a dozen years before him, but was as active in the business as he had ever been before. "Curtis Rochards," he requested, tying into the Brain Bank's operator.

When the racer-turned-agent came on the line, Raybo murmured quickly, "Yo, Curtis. I'll keep it short. You know the young racer Rev wanted me to check on? Well, I've checked his simulator scores and his studies, and I've met him, and I think the Rev's right. This is one we should help out. I'd like you to talk to MIDNITE and see what you can line up. . . ."

CHAPTER 8

The next few weeks passed quickly. Jass returned from one freight haul and departed on another. Mike's initial hopes for a quick reorganization of Jass's team were dwindling. It looked as though it would be a lengthy fund-raising process for Jass; he had one or two investors interested, but none willing to put up as much money as he needed. Mike occasionally ran into his old crewmates—Andy was now working for a factory team, also—but on his off-hours Mike was mostly alone with his library studies and the occasional simulator run. The encounter with Speedball Raybo had given a boost to his enthusiasm; but the glow couldn't last forever, and he had to look within himself for the determination to keep studying.

Mike got along well enough with most of his groundcrew mates on Stuart's team, but not really to the point of becoming friends with them. He sensed a certain standoffishness among the crew; many of them seemed a little jealous or defensive of their positions. Mike missed the easy camaraderie of Jass's crew. Stuart himself paused once in a while to greet him and offer a word of encouragement, but the pit manager who was Mike's direct boss was not so accommodating. Mike never knew his real name, but everyone called him Crackerjack. The man seemed oblivious to the feelings of any other sentient being and ordered Mike about as though he were just one more public-service automaton. Mike bore it, even when

Crackerjack became unreasonably demanding, but Mike kept his fingers crossed as he held his tongue.

At least he was learning, and saving a little money. But he soon became restless. How long could anyone with half a brain do nothing but sweep floors before he started to go bananas?

What rescued him from boredom was the upcoming Five-Star race, which put the whole crew into a state of excitement. Even the so-called "junior" pilots (who were pretty senior from Mike's point of view) began pitching in to help ready the *XTP Champion*, the three-drive brute that Stuart and his backup pilot, Scatt Dentmann, would be flying. On the day of the qualifying trials, Mike was asked to come in early; but during the actual flight, he was free to relax and enjoy the race.

Whereas Jass's crew had crowded into a tiny shack to see the racing monitors, the XTP crew—those without immediate duties, anyway—gathered in a comfortable lounge along with spouses, girlfriends, boyfriends, and some Poldavian friends. An array of big-screen monitors let everyone watch not only their own ship but the races in general. There was a distinctly festive atmosphere, which disappeared only briefly when a glitch delayed getting the *Champion* out of its dock. The techs solved the problem quickly; and then Stuart and Dentmann were off and running.

There was little worry over whether they would qualify—they were among the top-rated racers—and after a while, Mike began to focus on the other racers, to check out the competition. He became so involved, in fact, that he didn't even notice Speedball Raybo's appearance until he heard the name being murmured by the person next to him. Mike turned to look. Sure enough, at the back of the lounge, talking to one of the backers, was a floating silver-based PV with chevron patterns rippling through its energy field. Mike stared for a moment, then forced himself to look back at the screens. He couldn't very well just walk up and interrupt them to say hi, could he?

The *XTP Champion* was well on its way to an easy win in the qualifying run when Mike felt a tap on his shoulder. He turned. The slender black arm of Speedball Raybo was retracting as the automaton glided slowly past. Raybo's energy field flickered as he murmured, "What ho, Mike. Good race?"

Mike's mouth opened. "Yeah, terrific!" he said, grinning suddenly.

"Good. Glad you're enjoying it." Speedball didn't pause, but continued his glide right out the door. Mike gazed after him for a moment, blinking, and turned back to the races, basking in the knowledge that at least Raybo had remembered him.

And that, he thought, would keep him going for at least another week.

As it turned out, he didn't have much time to think about Raybo, or anything else except the team, for the next few days. Once the qualifying runs were over, the next event was the Five-Star race itself, and that was a much bigger event, since the best scorers from the trials would be coming together in head-to-head competition. Crackerjack whipped his crew into a near frenzy. Everything had to be just so, and heaven help the pitworker who mislaid a tool, or left a finger-smudge on or near the *XTP Champion*. The effect was contagious. Even workers who ordinarily had little to say to one another began reprimanding and cajoling each other.

It was in the midst of all this that Mike got a message from Jass, saying that he was back in Pitfall and had some information to pass on. Could Mike meet him for dinner?

He had to beg an extra hour off from Crackerjack, but finally Mike arranged to meet Jass at a crowded cafe in the outer racing ring. "Are you getting your team back together again?" he asked hopefully.

"Afraid not," Jass said. "Actually, I've taken a job for a couple of months instructing at the Pitfall Racing Academy—teaching young hoodlums like you the basics of the business."

Mike laughed. "Should I apply?"

Jass shook his head. "Nah. Most of the best racers

come out of the school of experience, not the academy. Anyway, you already know more than half the graduates, and the tuition is enough to give you the shakes.''

"Ah."

"Besides, I have something better to tell you."

Mike raised his eyebrows.

Jass gazed at him and smiled. "How would you like to be considered for a pilot's apprenticeship?"

Mike tensed. "Are you *kidding?*"

"Nope." Jass scratched the back of his head. "It's the oddest thing, too." He cocked his head and studied Mike. "I have a friend, an up-and-coming young pilot by the name of Lek Croveen. I don't know if I ever mentioned him before. He's had his own money problems. But he's just gotten some investor backing, so he's about to start doing some racing in earnest. And he's looking for someone to train as an apprentice and relief pilot."

"Wow," Mike said softly. He took a breath. "Do you think I'd have a shot at it? There are an awful lot of people—"

"Well, now, that's what's odd." Jass squinted. "When Lek told me about it, I mentioned your name—and would you believe, he'd heard of you already? What have you been *doing* that you've already got a reputation around here?"

Mike's breath escaped in an astonished laugh. He shrugged, dumbfounded.

"It seems your name was flagged on a list that he got from the central computer. Have you been doing some bang-up work on the simulators, or what? It takes most guys years to get listed."

Mike closed his eyes and opened them again. Finally he croaked, "Wow. I don't know. I hope the rating was good."

"Good enough that he wants to set up an interview." Jass raised a cautioning hand. "Now, don't get your hopes too fired up. He's going to talk to four or five people—so you're not the only prospect. But . . . I think you've got a shot at it. When can you see him?"

Mike grimaced. The timing couldn't have been more awkward. "Well, anytime. I mean . . ." He winced. "Actually, I'm not sure."

"You aren't thinking of playing hard to get, are you?" Jass asked with a frown. "He wants to find someone right away."

"*Good Lord, no.* It's just that . . . well, they've got me practically living at Rev's docks until after the big race. I suppose I could back out, but they'd be pretty mad."

Jass shook his head vigorously. "Uh-uh. Don't. Not if you've made a commitment. But can you squeeze an hour for an interview? Lek will understand that you're committed until after the race. But the sooner you talk to him, the better."

"I'll check," Mike promised. "As soon as I can."

"Great. Now hurry up and get back to work before your boss thinks you're out looking for another job!"

Crackerjack looked at Mike as though he had proposed treason. Mike repeated that he simply had urgent personal business to conduct. The pit manager scowled, but finally allowed that they could probably get along without him for an hour. Mike thanked him, and glanced up to see Fast Rev Stuart watching the exchange out of the corner of his eye. Stuart smiled faintly and turned away.

The following afternoon, he made his way down the dock row to the lower-budget section, not far from where Jass had been based. Despite his nervousness about the interview, Mike felt a certain relief in coming back down here; it was funkier and more relaxed after the formality of the better-heeled racing community. He felt more at home. Once he found Lek Croveen's dock, however, his pulse started to rise again.

There was no racing ship in sight, just an empty dock. Maybe the ship was out on a trial run. He didn't ask, but went directly to the office, noting the small hand-lettered sign that said, simply CROVEEN'S TEAM. As he was going in, a young redheaded woman was just leaving.

Behind her stood a tall blond man who looked to be in his early twenties. His expression was serious as he saw Mike. "Are you Mike Murray?"

"Yes, I—"

"Lek Croveen." Lek stuck out his hand. "Glad to meet you." He turned. "This is Twyla Rogres. She's interviewing for a position as well. Twyla, Mike."

The two shook hands warily. Twyla was Mike's height and a couple of years older, with greenish-gold eyes and a streak of emerald in her flame-red hair. She studied Mike for a moment, with what seemed a measured expression of distrust. Finally she said, "Glad to meet you. Good luck." But it sounded as though she meant "Good luck somewhere else."

"I'll be in touch, Twyla," Lek said. She nodded and left. "Come on in, Mike."

Mike followed Lek into the office, wondering about Twyla. He decided not to mention the encounter; instead he asked about the ship, or rather the lack of a ship, in the dock.

Lek laughed ruefully. "You noticed that, did you? Don't worry, we have a racer. But it's out in the vacuum dock. We've got a defective airscreen generator, and until we get it fixed, we have to keep the steel airdoors closed, and we can't bring the ship in. Jass may have told you—we've just gotten backing, and we're hoping for a slot in the big Sam Adams race coming up a little ways down the road. But our cash flow is still pretty tight."

"Ah-ha." Mike was getting used to hearing that, in one version or another. But the Sam Adams—that was a biggie, in the Three Star category. He was impressed; quite impressed.

"So tell me a little about yourself," Lek said. "You want to become an apprentice . . ."

Mike described his experience to date, which admittedly wasn't much, a fact that Lek's response seemed to confirm. When he went on to explain his simulator training and his other studies, however, Lek's ears perked up. Lek seemed impressed by Mike's efforts, at least, and the more he probed, tossing out theoretical questions, the better Mike sounded. Or so Mike thought; and Lek's expression, as he placed a finger to his lips, seemed encouraging.

They talked for the better part of an hour, before Mike realized with a start that he was due back at work. He took a deep breath, not wanting to interrupt Lek's description of his plans for his team. Mike nodded in answer to a question about whether he'd be ready to put in the time and commitment that Lek required, and stammered, "Yes, uh . . ."

Lek cocked his head. "Is there a problem?"

"No, it's just . . ." Mike glanced at the time again. "I'm supposed to be back at the Rev's dock. They only gave me an hour off, and they're really crazy now with the race coming up."

Lek stood. "Oh, well, why didn't you say so? We don't want you to lose your old job just yet." He stuck out his hand. "I'll talk to you again in a few days."

They shook hands. "Well—I hope—" Mike coughed. "I mean, thanks for talking."

"Good luck to your boss in the race. I'll be watching that one," Lek said as he ushered Mike out.

"I'll tell him," Mike promised. But as he walked away, he realized that he couldn't, or shouldn't, mention his interview to anyone until after the race. And by then, he hoped, he'd have his answer.

And his luck had been so good up to this point, could it possibly desert him now?

As it turned out, the decision of whether or not to mention his interview was taken out of his hands. Crackerjack was eyeing him as he returned to his job fifteen minutes late. Though Mike took a bit of razzing from the other pitworkers about his "long lunch," he didn't think much about it—until Crackerjack called him into his office, an hour before quitting time.

"Well, now," said the pit manager, in a none-too-kind voice. Mike swallowed. "We missed you, this afternoon. Thought you said you were going to be back in an hour.''

Mike nodded. ''I'm sorry. I . . . it took a little longer than I thought it would.''

Crackerjack seemed to be staring past Mike, through the little office window. ''Uh-huh,'' he said after a moment.

''The guys were able to cover for me,'' Mike said. ''I don't think there was any problem.''

The pit manager's eyes flicked sideways to meet his, and at that moment, Mike knew that he was in trouble. He'd known all along that Crackerjack didn't much like him—seemed to think he was too ambitious for a kid—but for the first time, Mike sensed real anger. Over a lousy fifteen minutes?

''*Was* there a problem?'' Mike asked reluctantly.

Crackerjack replied with a point-blank question. ''What were you doing this afternoon?'' Mike blinked. ''Are you looking for another job?''

Mike's breath failed him. He hadn't expected to be confronted so quickly, or so directly. Had he done something wrong? He didn't think so. But . . .

''Well?''

Mike cleared his throat quickly. ''I was talking to someone, yes. There's a possibility of an apprenticeship . . .''

His boss scowled. ''An apprenticeship?''

''Yes, to be an apprentice pilot.'' Mike looked back at his boss for a moment in puzzlement. Was Crackerjack just dense—or was he being intentionally dense? ''This just opened up and I needed to talk to the pilot right away.'' He hesitated, then figured that he might as well be completely up-front. ''It's what I've been looking to do since I got here, and—''

''You *know* we're shorthanded for this race coming up, a very *important* race—don't you?'' his boss snapped.

''I—'' Mike's voice caught. Shorthanded? They were busy, yes; but shorthanded? Mike didn't think so. ''I wasn't thinking of leaving before the race,'' he managed finally. ''It's not like I would—''

His boss sniffed and looked out the window again.

Mike's voice trailed off. There was a moment of awful silence before Crackerjack, with a gesture of dismissal, said, "All right. We'll need you to work late tonight. I trust you'll give us a week's warning before you go."

"Sure," Mike croaked, rising. There was no response, nor did Crackerjack meet his gaze again as Mike turned and left.

He knew he shouldn't; but when the other guys started asking what was going on, Mike hemmed and hawed, and finally muttered that he'd been to a job interview. As a result, he had to put up with even more razzing for the rest of the day—which might not have been so bad if it hadn't been for good old Jake.

Jake was a pit mechanic, and Jake had been riding him mercilessly for about twenty minutes, arguing that if they were going to give Mike a job as a pilot, they must be hiring right out of finishing school these days. Whereas most of the pitmen were good-natured in their teasing, Jake had a chip on his shoulder, as usual. Jake prided himself on his lack of formal education. In truth, he was quite good at his job, a natural mechanic who had learned his craft with his hands. Unfortunately, he took every opportunity to knock down anyone who took a more "learned" approach to the racing business. And this time his target was Mike. "Hey, schoolboy!" he taunted.

Mike responded with stoic silence, though inwardly he was seething. He knew that anything he could say would only make it worse, so he held his tongue. But he reached his limit when Jake made a derogatory reference to his parents. Mike let fly with an oily rag. "Listen!" he snapped. "Just because you're too damn . . . *dumb* to want to do anything more in this world . . ." He glared, his heart pounding with resentment. "Just *get off my back!*"

The mechanic slowly wiped his face where the rag had struck him. His eyes were filled with rage. "You little swine! You come in here sweeping floors, and you think all of a sudden you're fit to tell us what to do? Because

you had one interview? Because Speedball Raybo likes
you?''

Mike's face must have shown his surprise, because
Jake added with a sneer, "You think nobody saw you
cozying up to him last race?" He moved forward
threateningly. "You think you're pretty hot stuff, don't
you?''

Mike backed away fearfully; then something in him
tightened and he stood his ground. "No, I don't think I'm
hot stuff," he said, his voice trembling. "But I don't think
you are, either." Mike knew he was no streetfighter; but if
the time came . . .

"Hey, guys—cut it out, will you?" said one of the
other mechanics, stepping between the two.

"I'll cut the little swine's *tongue* out," Jake growled.

"If you try anything—" Mike muttered.

"That's enough!" The flat twang of Crackerjack's
voice cut through the hangar. Mike looked up and saw the
pit manager stalking across the dock. "What's going on
here?" Crackerjack crossed his arms and glared at the two,
his tongue pushed down into his lower lip so that it looked
as though he had a plug of tobacco in his mouth.

Mike started to speak, but Crackerjack cut him off. "I
didn't ask you. Jake—what's going on?"

Jake shrugged and turned away. "Nothin'. This guy
was just spouting off about his great new career, that's
all.''

Mike stared after him in astonishment, before turning
to Crackerjack. "I was not—"

"Come with me," Crackerjack snapped, walking
away.

Mike followed, exchanging a helpless glance with the
pitworker who had tried to break up the argument. He felt
a knot in his stomach as he walked into the pit office.
Crackerjack stood with his back to Mike. "What were you
trying to do, start a fight there?" Before Mike could
answer, he turned. "I don't need troublemakers in my
dock," he growled. "I especially don't need them three
days before a race. Got that?"

"But I—"

"Shut up." Crackerjack squinted out the window. "I don't care what happened back there." His gaze snapped back to Mike. "I don't *care*. I don't need it here and I don't want it. So you're out."

Mike stared at him open-mouthed. "What!"

"I'm a fair man," Crackerjack said. "We'll call it a personality conflict. We won't say anything about you shooting your mouth off about *another racing team*—right when we need team spirit and cooperation. So pick up your pay at the end of the week—and until then stay out of here."

"But I *didn't*—"

The manager's eyes blazed. "I don't want to hear it. Now get out."

Mike was too stunned to protest. He wouldn't have known what to say, anyway—not in the face of this. Exhaling slowly, he turned—and walked out of the office and out of Crackerjack's dock without speaking to another person.

The next two days were a blur of misery, mitigated only by his hopes for an apprenticeship with Lek. But he didn't know when he would hear—probably not for a few more days. Until then, all he could think of was that he had blown his one and only chance at making it here in Pitfall. Never mind that he didn't know what he'd done wrong! He hadn't done anything, except work at a job with a jealous coworker and a boss who wouldn't listen to reason.

Was this how the real world worked? If so, what was the point of trying? It wasn't fair; he'd come all the way from Earth, risking everything. For this?

He wished he'd never come.

He told Jass about it over dinner. He didn't really feel like talking about it, but he had to tell someone. Jass listened, nodding sympathetically. He didn't seem shocked. It was, he said, the sort of thing that happened; sooner or later, no matter who you were, you were going to run into

104

someone who didn't like you, for whatever reason. There wasn't much you could do except grit your teeth and carry on, especially if the other person held the authority.

That wasn't very reassuring. What Mike wanted to hear was that he had been subjected to a terrible injustice, and that there was something he could do about it.

He'd thought of going directly to Rev Stuart, but Jass counseled him against it. "In the first place," Jass said, flagging down a waiter for more coffee, "you're going to leave soon anyway, if Lek gives you the nod. Right?"

"Well, yes, but—"

"And in the second place, there are certain protocols you have to observe in those big factory teams. Hierarchies of authority." Jass stabbed a finger at the table. "Now, the pit manager usually runs his own shop. He's in charge of his own people. Even a senior racer like Stuart will defer to him in personnel matters. So, Rev might have the *power* to overrule Crackerjack, but if he does, he'll be creating other problems for himself. And I don't think he needs that now."

Mike nodded sullenly, feeling the rage build up inside him all over again. "It just doesn't seem fair," he complained.

Jass shrugged. "Did anybody promise you *fair*?"

To that, Mike had no answer. Nor did he think of any answer over the next two days. There was no word from Lek, and he couldn't bring himself to look for another job right now. He holed up in cafes during the day, nursing cups of coffee or tea and wishing miserably that he would bump into someone, anyone, perhaps a big-name racer, who would recognize him and offer him a partnership. Terrific pipe dream. He knew he shouldn't even be spending as much money as he was, but somehow knowing that made it even harder to conserve; he found himself ordering snacks that he didn't need, almost by reflex, to make himself feel better.

The day he went in to pick up his termination pay was race day. He avoided the pit area, not wanting to see or be seen by his former coworkers. Coming out of the office, though, he could not resist the lounge, where a crowd was already gathered to watch the race. He stood for a few moments at the back of the room, watching the images on the large screens as the heavy racing ships moved into position near the outer shell of Pitfall. In the web, moving flares of colored light marked the racers in a AA-class warm-up race that was going on now, prior to the main event. Mike felt a lump growing in his throat as he thought of the excitement he should be sharing now with the rest of the crew. He turned and walked quickly away.

He just couldn't stay away altogether, though. Partway around the ring, he found a cafe with viewing screens and he watched the start of the race from there. He was drawn by fascination and anger. *Dammit, he should be a part of this.* In the end, he couldn't stand it; he got up and left in mid-race, and spent the next two hours wandering sullenly through the dock areas, poking his head into commissaries once in a while to check and see who was winning. Stuart was in fourth position, but if he was going to pull into the lead, he would have to do it soon. Time was running out, and the first three racers were hanging tough as they looped around the sun, keeping him from passing.

The Rev never did succeed in moving up past third. Mike watched the final lap sadly, standing at the back of a noisy snack-bar crowd, craning his neck at a too-small screen that showed the blips of colored light whizzing past the orbiting grandstands. The shot cut to the leader's nose-camera as it flashed by the finish, and yells of approval and disappointment went up from the crowd. Mike let out a long, deep sigh and went home.

It took the better part of twenty-four hours for Mike to convince himself that he had not somehow sabotaged the Rev's race by creating dissension and bad spirit among the crew. So he was feeling more than a little low already when he returned from a long walk the next day to find an electronic mail note from Lek Croveen awaiting him at the rooming house.

His heart jumped. Then he read the note:

Mike: This is to let you know that I've selected Twyla Rogres for the position of apprentice pilot with my team. You are a fine candidate, and it is only because of her greater experience that I chose Twyla. I wish that I could somehow take on both of you, but at my current level of backing, I can't. Best of luck finding a spot with another team. Lek.

Mike stood, white-faced, in the tiny lobby of the rooming house. The superintendent was sitting behind his desk, watching him. "Hey, is anything wrong?"

Mike stared at him without seeing, through a blur of tears. He didn't, couldn't, answer.

CHAPTER 9

Days passed, one just like another.

Mike had never been so low. The loss of Jass's team had been a disappointment, to be sure, but nothing compared to this. Now he felt as though all hope were gone. He would never get a recommendation from the Rev's crew—not with Crackerjack in charge. It was just so unfair! He wanted to yell, to lash out, to *hurt* someone; and then, in the next moment, he wanted to do nothing more than curl up and disappear.

He did little except sleep and walk around Pitfall, barely registering what he was seeing. He began staying up late and waking up late, sometimes not venturing out of his room until midafternoon. Jass was tied up with his teaching duties, so Mike really was alone. He thought of going to the library to study, but the idea seemed repellent now. What was the point of cramming knowledge that he was never going to get a chance to use?

What was the point in having come to Clypsis in the first place? If there was no more justice in the world than this, what chance was there of fulfilling his dream? There was nothing worse than futility, and futility was what he was up against. Face it, he thought. You had it and you blew it.

For the first time in a while, he thought longingly of Earth and his friends on the docks there—he'd never gotten around to writing to tell them how he was doing, and there was little point in doing so now. And he thought chokingly of his Aunt Anna. If there was to have been one good outcome of her unfair and untimely death, it was that it had gotten him off Earth and on his way to the racing career he'd longed for since he was a boy. (Well, okay— but he was *almost* an adult. He hurt inside enough to be an adult.) And now?

The days passed, but they seemed like months, years. His savings dwindled, and once more he faced the prospect of deportation if he didn't find work. But he couldn't seem to make himself look. He wasn't quite broke yet; he'd look when he had to.

In time, he found his way back to The Wugbug. Alyson Avery and Crystal Cashe were performing again, which was some consolation, though not much. He sat as far in the back as he could, listening to the music and studying the patterns of lights in the ceiling. The music at first irritated him more than it soothed, and he sighed when the rest of the audience applauded. He was almost glad when the set ended and he could sit in peace, feeling sorry for himself without distraction. He didn't even know why he'd come in here. He thought of leaving; but where would he go?

When the singers returned, a little later, he watched them glumly as they stepped into the lights. He thought he saw Crystal glance his way for an instant, but when she began to introduce the first song of the new set, she was looking toward the center of the audience. Therefore, he was more than a little surprised when she said, "We'd like to open this set with a special song for a friend of ours. He's sitting way in the back, and we hope this cheers him up." She turned and gazed straight at Mike with a friendly smile. Behind her, Alyson waved cheerily, and from her board came a loud, rattling drum riff. Mike blushed in the darkness, and then the two launched into their song, and it was the one he had heard weeks ago: "*Ngikutzandza . . .*"

I love you . . .

By the time they were finished and on to their next song, Mike was not only swallowing back an enormous lump in his throat, he was feeling positively ashamed—as well as awed, comforted, infatuated, embarrassed, and probably a dozen other things all at once. The embarrassment was almost enough to make him get up and leave, but his legs refused to work, and he wound up just sitting there, grinning like a lovelorn sap. What are you *grinning* about? he asked himself. What do you have to be *happy* about? And another voice in him answered, You idiot, they just dedicated a song to you—they *like* you—so where do you get off with the self-pity?

When the final set ended, the two singers strode off the stage with a flourish. They waved to Mike, and he returned the wave giddily as they bounded up the aisle and disappeared into the dressing rooms.

And that, he decided as he came slowly back to reality, was his cue to take off. Besides, there was some work that he had to do, work that he was getting more than a little behind on.

He greeted Browser MacPhee sheepishly. He was surprised to see Browser in the library at this hour—didn't the man ever take time off?—but Browser looked even more surprised to see Mike. "Well, hello! I was beginning to wonder if we'd lost you," MacPhee said as Mike pressed his wrist to the identiscanner. He looked at Mike quizzically.

"Nope." Mike was glad to be back, but he didn't want to talk about it. "Got a terminal for me?"

Browser grinned and gestured expansively. The library was deserted. "I think we can scare one up for you."

Mike chose a terminal and set to work at once. There was a lot he had to learn about warp-field mechanics. . . .

It was deep in the night, and the racing offices were quiet when Speedball Raybo placed the conference call first to MIDNITE and then to Curtis Rochards. Raybo hummed with thought as he waited for MIDNITE to respond to his call.

"Yo, MIDNITE," Raybo said, as the connection opened.

"Well past midnight, I'm afraid," answered the Master of Integrated Data Network and Intelligence Transfer Engineer, who also happened to be the Chairman of the Racing Commission. He also happened to be a computer program, but that didn't mean he didn't have a sense of humor.

"Well, as long as we're both up anyway, let's talk business, shall we?" Raybo let his colors swirl in a pattern that he knew MIDNITE would recognize as a good-natured grin. "Think you can pull Curtis away from his wheeling and dealing long enough to talk to us?"

"Well, since I was the one he was wheeling and dealing *with*, until you interrupted us, I think I can manage," MIDNITE said. "Hold the line a moment."

It was more like a nanosecond before the agent Curtis Rochards said, "Raybo, I've been looking for you. What's this I hear about your man finally coming out of his shell and buckling down to work?"

"Indeed," said MIDNITE. "He was logged into the library for three hours tonight."

"I told you he'd come around," Raybo said. "When Rev Stuart and I recommend someone, we usually don't make mistakes."

There was a ripple of laughter from the others. "No?" Rochards said. "What about that young Merkek you wanted us to back who—"

"I said *usually*. I didn't say *never*. Anyway, you can't expect the kid not to have gone through a rough time. Not after what Crackerjack pulled on him."

"True enough. I had to argue with Stuart not to get involved himself," Rochards said. "Anyway, now we know the kid has some guts. He took it hard, but he bounced back."

"So. The question remains: Can we get another investor in on this deal?"

MIDNITE answered first. "Based on what I've seen,

I'd rate both the team and Murray as A-minus risks, for a small-to-medium investment.''

"That's pretty good, coming from you, you old codger,'' Raybo said. "I'm surprised you ever rate anyone higher than a B.''

"I'm not sure that the word *codger* applies, coming from someone who—''

"If you two could knock it off for a minute,'' Rochards interrupted, "I'd like to offer a point of information.'' There was a polite silence."Thank you. Now, I've already been in touch with the Frank L. James syndicate, and they're ready, on our recommendation, to commit ten thousand interstellar yen to the team on top of what Dietrich and Dagio have put in.''

Raybo would have blinked if he'd had eyes. "Just like that?''

"Well, I've kept them informed, and they trust your recommendation.'' The nonincarnate Rykell chuckled. "Now, I just hope you're right about his potential.''

"Oh, I do, too,'' Raybo said. "Can you handle it? Shall we consider it done?''

"Think of it as done,'' Rochards answered.

It was the fourth straight day that Mike had come home empty-handed from job-hunting without so much as a breath of encouragement. He was willing to do anything; sweeping floors would have seemed a luxury. But he was beginning to wonder: Had Crackerjack put out the word that the Murray kid was a troublemaker and not to be trusted? It was so discouraging to have doors slammed in his face, over and over! But his determination had been renewed; and anyway, he still had his evenings to spend in the library, and he was throwing himself into his studies as never before.

On returning to his room, he was so bone-tired that he almost failed to notice the message light. As he was peeling off his shirt for a shower, he stared at the tiny winking light for a moment before its meaning penetrated.

Message, he thought. Probably Jass. I haven't called him; he wants to know if I'm alive.

He was too beat to talk to Jass now. He continued undressing and went into the shower for a long, relaxing mist. By the time he came out, he was feeling somewhat more human, and very hungry. There was, however, the problem of where to eat, since his finances were practically nonexistent. Finally he decided to just walk to the nearest market and buy a loaf of bread to bring back to his room.

He was at the market when he remembered the message; then he forgot it again until he was returning through the rooming-house foyer. With a sigh, he sat on a tattered chair and chewed on a piece of heavy dark bread while he waited for the terminal to become available. When his fellow roomer finally cleared the screen and got up to leave, Mike took his place and stuck his wrist against the scanner.

To his surprise, the message wasn't from Jass. It was from Lek Croveen. Mike's breath caught; his eyes widened; his mouth opened as he began to read:

Mike: Pleased to report that I've received additional backing. Now possible for me to hire additional ground crew. It's not quite piloting, but good experience. Are you interested? Lek Croveen.

Mike stared at the screen for a full minute. A yell started to bubble up in his throat; he caught himself in mid-cry and glanced around self-consciously. With a huge grin he leaned forward to send a reply.

By the middle of the next day, he was on the job, feeling as though the last weeks had happened in another life. Lek immediately put him to work helping to program the tactical racing computer. That, in fact, was to be Mike's primary responsibility, though he would be working with other members of the ground crew as well, learning, among other things, fusion-reactor maintenance and repair. Lek seemed willing to give Mike all the responsibility he could handle, and Mike was eager to take it on.

Right now he was ready to take the world on.

Lek's crew was a friendly and hard-working bunch, more like Jass's crew than Crackerjack's. Lek was in there working, getting his hands dirty along with everyone else—and there was no pit manager other than Lek himself. The chief tactician was a burnt-looking Merkek humanoid named Andru, who, oddly enough, came with a British, educated-at-Cambridge accent, as well as a droll wit and a penchant for practical jokes. The primary fusion tech was a four-armed Polaran female named Dwaine, who seemed to have not just an intuitive, but almost a telepathic understanding of the reactors. According to Lek, she was half mechanic, half reactor psychiatrist. She forbore the use of mech assistants, swearing that only with her own fingers could she do the job right. No one argued with her. The only robots in the pit were for heavy lifting, welding, and cleaning.

The day before Mike's arrival on the team, they had gotten the airscreen generator repaired and had brought the racer, the *Slippery Cat*, into the pit. The *Cat* was a smaller ship than the *XTP Champion*, and longer and slimmer than Jass's *Silver Cannon*. She was painted in a flowing black-and-white pattern, with viewscreen sensors where the cat-eyes would be, and she looked ready at a moment's notice to leap and dash down the long tube of the warpweb. Mike was in love with her at first sight.

Mike's only problem, as it turned out, was Twyla Rogres, Lek's apprentice pilot. Mike wasn't sure why, but he and Twyla mixed like oil and water. At first, he found himself suppressing a twinge whenever he saw her, knowing that she had gotten the position that (he couldn't help thinking) might have been his. It wasn't that he was unhappy with his present job—he was overjoyed with it, and he was learning more than ever. And yet, he could never seem to talk to Twyla without one or the other of them somehow getting angry.

It didn't help that Twyla had a hair-trigger temper and

an intemperate tongue. One day she came aboard the *Cat* to find him programming into the computer some experimental tactical maneuvers that he, with Andru's help, had developed. He glanced up as she entered, but his thoughts were deep in the intricacies of the program, and he didn't say anything as she sat in the pilot's seat, gazing at him suspiciously.

"Aren't you going a little overboard, plugging that stuff in before you've tested it out on the simulator?" she asked. "Do Lek and Andru know you're doing that?"

Mike slowly focused his eyes on her, and his mind on what she had just said. "Of course they do," he answered, irritated not only by her comment, but also by the fact that she'd just made him lose his train of thought. "Anyway, you might have noticed that I haven't exactly had a lot of access to the simulator." As he said that, he regretted his tone. Twyla, after all, was the apprentice pilot, not he; and it was only natural that she had priority on the simulator.

Twyla did not fail to miss the sarcasm, whether regretted or not. Her brows arched, and she said, "Well, if *that's* the problem, let's you and I have a go at it tonight, and you can show me what you know." Her eyes danced with fire. "Since you have *so* much experience."

Flushing with anger and embarrassment, Mike accepted the challenge. And without another word, he turned back to his programming.

After an early dinner, Mike returned to find Twyla waiting impatiently by the simulator that Lek's team shared with three other teams. "I wasn't sure you were going to show," she said, with just enough of a smile that he thought it *might* be a joke. He took a silent breath and nodded. An apprentice pilot from one of the other teams emerged from the simulator, signed off, and departed with a wave. Mike gestured toward the door and followed Twyla into the simulator.

The cockpit looked enough like the real thing to create an illusion—though it wasn't hard, if one looked twice, to see that the panels were cheap plastic, and that many of the pipes and structural elements were obviously nonfunctional or missing altogether. Mike had been spoiled by the simulator for the *XTP Champion*, which was a virtual replica of the racer's cockpit. Still, it was the best way, short of actually flying, to gain experience. He closed the hatch as Twyla took up her place—in the primary pilot's seat, of course. Never mind, he thought. She can have it. The seat doesn't matter. What matters is the flying.

Twyla was busy setting up the flight program as he squeezed into the seat beside her. "We're going one-on-one," she said casually as he settled into place. As he nodded agreement, she was already pulling the divider closed between the two seats. "See you at the finish line," she added in a half-mocking tone. Then the divider snicked into place, cutting Mike off.

Okay, he thought, powering up his console in the tiny compartment. See you at the finish line. The program she'd called up altered the normal integrated configuration of the two consoles and pitted them against one another in simulated competition. He'd never done it this way—always before he'd been flying against the computer—but there was a first time for everything. Donning a helmet, he switched on the communicator and asked Twyla if she could hear him.

Twyla answered, "*Alley Cat* here. I read you. Ready to launch."

Alley cat? "*Junkyard Dog*," he answered. "Ready to launch."

He heard a faintly inhuman laughter in his headset, and was puzzled for a moment, because it sounded familiar, but it wasn't Twyla. Then he heard Andru's clipped Merkek voice, from the outside console. "Kennel Control here. Was just passing by and thought I'd check in. You gents want a monitor on your race?"

Twyla must have been as surprised as Mike, but she covered it well. "Sure thing, Kennel. I guess we could use a chaperon. But no funny stuff. This is a straight race. How about it, Junkyard?"

"Righto—ready," Mike said. "Keep us honest, Andru."

"Very well. Gentlemen, test your engines."

Mike snapped through the preliminaries quickly and kicked in his simulated engines. He felt a throb through his seat, almost—but not quite—like the real thing. The viewscreen showed an image of the Pitfall structure drifting slowly away. Beyond the structure was the distant wall, gridded with tiny lights. The throb of the engine test faded, and at Andru's signal, he piloted toward the entry circle. "On the green light, the race begins," he heard; and on his board, a moment later, a light flashed green and he hit the main drive and his seat shook with the vibration.

The spin-up circle swallowed him whole. Alongside him was the image of Twyla's *Alley Cat*. The groove at the beginning was wide enough for both of them, but soon enough it began to narrow, and the jockeying for position began. Mike rode his throttle carefully, mindful not only of his fuel and engine pressures, but also of the value of getting the lead position at the start. At the back of his mind was the knowledge of how much more unbearable Twyla would become if he lost to her.

The tube ahead glimmered and narrowed—and Twyla was beginning to edge ahead to his left—she was being a trifle more daring than he.

"Five seconds to main ring, animals," he heard Andru say.

"Eat dust, Earthman!" Twyla cried with a wicked laugh, rocketing forward at full thrust.

"Why, I'll—" he started to answer, then shut up. Biting his lower lip, he redlined his throttle and held it. Swinging into Twyla's exhaust, he opened his ramscoop to full efficiency and leaped after her. He gained quickly—but too late! The warptube narrowed, and she hit the groove just ahead of him, at transfactor three. He swung wide to pass and hit turbulence. Grimly he bucked through it, shaking, hoping to get around her before his engine overflared; but she was keeping *Alley Cat* redlined, too, and she was in the track of the smoothest, fastest-moving stream of space. She pulled away from him slowly but inexorably.

Cursing to himself, he swung back into the groove behind her and eased back on the throttle to save his engines. "What's the matter, Junkdog?" he heard her taunting in his headphones.

He pulled into position to take advantage of her wake. He stayed close on her tail and didn't answer.

"*Junkyard Dog* getting old?" she called.

Still he didn't answer. He was thinking furiously. He could only follow and wait for an opportunity to get by her. He heard Andru calling out the lap-points, counting their progress as the two imaginary racers whirled around the sun. It was a short, three-lap race, and he didn't have a lot of time to figure out a way to pass.

Finally he heard one last taunt from Twyla: "*Alley Cat* saying good-bye! Don't get lost, *Junkyard*!" Her engines flared to full thrust again, and she leaped away from him.

Mike was only an instant behind, and he had the advantage of her drag and her exhaust. He kept his engines just shy of the red danger line—dogging her tail—while she pushed her drivers to their limit. "Think I'm gonna get a taste of cat fur!" he murmured aloud as he closed in on her again.

Andru droned, "Final lap, third point . . ."

Mike redlined and swung hard. He passed the velocity shear cleanly this time and hit the passing lane at top acceleration. He smiled to himself as he slipped even with Twyla and slowly edged out in front. His engines were in the danger zone now, but he didn't have the clearance yet to hit the groove ahead of her. The passing zone was slower than the groove; it took extra power just to match speeds, and more power yet to get around a ship in the groove. Praying that his engines would hold, he kept up the pressure and watched Twyla gradually losing on him. She must have already pushed her engines too hard . . .

"Final lap, last point . . . Mike, your meters are way into the red zone . . ."

Drawing a sharp breath, Mike swung toward the

118

groove. It was close . . . he hit the turbulence and rocked and shot into the groove *right* in front of Twyla, swinging back and forth as he tried to regain stability . . . but he'd done it, he was in the lead and the finish was coming up in seconds—

His console went red right across the board, and he felt a tremendous shaking under his seat, which faded away . . . *What the devil was happening?*

The viewscreen flashed white.

He heard Andru groaning and Twyla cursing bitterly, and the realization slowly reached him of what he had done.

"Oh, Mike, come back to us, Mike!" Andru sang mournfully. "Mike, we knew ye well. Did ye have to take Twyller with ye?"

The console cleared, reset. Mike sighed, dropping his hands into his lap. Only then did he realize that he was shaking. He took a deep breath and finally found his voice and murmured, "So—" His voice cracked and he cleared his throat. "So, what happened, anyway?"

The dividing screen slid open, and Twyla glared at him from the next seat. "What happened?" she growled. "You just killed me, and probably yourself as well, that's what happened." She hooked her thumb toward the hatch. "Andru will tell you."

Mike blinked as he staggered out of the simulator, followed by the feisty redhead. Andru was waiting, the slightest wisp of a smile showing on his sunburned face. He extended a thin, bony hand. "Welcome back from the dead," he murmured. He shook Twyla's hand after Mike's. "You blew your engines, sir. Blew them up right in Twyla's face, as a matter of fact."

Mike blanched and glanced at Twyla. She had her hands on her hips, glaring at him. Mike cleared his throat. "Sorry," he murmured. Trying desperately to lighten the moment, he added, "But I did get around you."

Andru ducked away from Twyla's outburst: "*You what—you idiot—what do you think this is!*"

After Twyla ran out of breath, Andru said, chuckling,

"It's not good form to *kill* your rival, Mike. I don't believe the panel can award you that one, even posthumously."

Mike nodded, hanging his head. "Right," he muttered. Finally he took a deep breath and met Twyla's eyes. He extended his hand and swallowed. "Your race," he said softly.

Twyla grinned and snorted, slapped his hand, and walked out of the room. Mike sighed and turned back to Andru. "Monitor me in another run?" he asked sheepishly.

"Kennel Control, at your service," Andru answered.

CHAPTER 10

In the days that followed, Mike kept to his work and Twyla kept to hers, and little was said about the simulation session. Mike's performances improved—when he could get time in the simulator. At least, he never made the same mistake again, and he made a point of exploring just how far one could push these engines, not only without their blowing up and killing someone, but without their being seriously damaged. It was no victory to win a race if one's engines were ruined in the process. The replacement cost could easily exceed the purse in many of the smaller races.

During the second week, the team came together for some pre-race practice flights for Lek and Twyla in the *Slippery Cat*. Mike worked closely with Andru in programming the tactical computers, which they would be monitoring from the pit. Mike and Andru's new maneuvering program was due for a trial, and they spent a couple of hours going over it with the pilots. Twyla was clearly skeptical; but as Lek seemed content to give it a try, she said nothing, at least not during the meeting.

Flight day arrived, and Mike took his place in front of a console as the *Cat* was rolled out and set free. He felt his usual twinge of envy, but struggled to keep his thoughts on his job. Ground-to-ship talk muttered around him as the ship made its way out toward the spin-up ring and the web. Mike and the rest of the ground crew watched as Lek put the ship through her paces. Then Twyla took over.

Lek had run the experimental program first. He'd

found a few minor bugs but reported it basically workable. Twyla had more trouble. The intent of the program was to assist the pilot in swinging the ship from side to side in the groove, creating turbulence in the drag and exhaust effects to slow a pursuer, without slowing himself too much. The program had a limited but important application—to help maintain an edge against a single close pursuer. It involved some sacrifice of speed in return for costing the opponent (one hoped) even more speed. The trick was to coordinate the program with one's other maneuvers; applying override at the wrong time could cause self-defeating turbulence and a loss of power. It was the coordination that was causing Twyla problems.

"Ground," she reported, "I'm getting too damn much swing. Can't you tune this thing down a little?"

Mike saw the problem on the screen—and the cause, as well. She was overcompensating for the program's movements. Lek was letting her fly it her way, letting her solve the problem herself—except that she wasn't. She needed to ease off. Mike reached to cut himself into the circuit. "If you—"

Andru's warning hand cut off his intended remark. Mike looked up and saw the tactician shaking his frizzy-haired head. Andru took the circuit. "We copy, Twyla. Cut the program out for a minute and give us a chance to reset. We'll send you the numbers."

"Okay." There was a hiss of static for a moment, then Twyla's voice cut in again. "Thank heavens, it's off."

Mike shot Andru a questioning glance. The tactician ignored him until he'd gotten the revised numbers to Twyla. When she reported verification, he said, "Cut it back in when you're ready." Then he turned and said to Mike, "When the pilot asks for a change in the programming, and you can do it without risking the ship, you do it." He looked as though he wanted to say more, but then Twyla was back on the circuit with a description of what was happening. Mike listened.

"All right, it's damped," Twyla said. "But now

we're not shaking up the wake enough to do any good. How much longer do you want me to keep trying this?"

Andru answered, "Quit whenever you're ready. We can go over the results on this later."

Mike frowned. She hadn't really given it a fair trial. "Okay, it's off," Twyla said.

A moment later, they heard Lek's voice. "Time to go to passing maneuvers. On my mark, send us a ghost."

Andru answered, "One ghost, coming right up."

By the time they were ready for post-flight analysis, Mike was confident that he could explain at least some of the problems that Twyla had encountered. She and Lek had spent half an hour chasing "ghosts," computerized images projected onto their screens to simulate other ships running in the web with them. Several times Mike had seen Twyla swing too wide in passing, losing speed at the edge of the racing tube, where the warp effect fell to its minimum. She was crossing the velocity shear from the groove to the passing lane too slowly, and, as a result, oversteering as she bucked through the turbulence.

No one seemed to be addressing the problem at the debriefing, so when Lek threw the meeting open to discussion, Mike took a deep breath and raised his hand. "Sure, Mike," Lek said. "What have you got?"

"Well, I think I know why you were having some problems there, when you were passing—Twyla, I mean." He hesitated and cleared his throat. "It's the same thing you were doing when we had the tacticals running." As he spoke, he was dimly aware of the others stirring in reaction—Lek raising one eyebrow, Twyla scowling, Andru wincing. But he was already started, and his mind was trying to get the words right and the explanation straight, and he wasn't paying attention to how his teammates were reacting.

When he finished, he stopped for breath and then looked at the others. Andru was staring off into space, not moving a muscle or meeting anyone's gaze; and Lek's expression, he couldn't quite read. He looked at Twyla.

Her eyes were filled with fire. "I'm glad," she said, her voice razor-sharp, "that you know so much about it. Undoubtedly it's a result of your vast experience in flying real ships, not simulations. Far superior to my own experience." Her eyes flashed around the room. "In case there's any mistake, let me just explain to everyone that I am quite well aware of the problem of oversteering and—"

"Twyla, wait," Lek said.

"—that was the *whole damn point*—"

"Twyla!"

"—of this practice exercise. Repeating the obvious is not helpful. What would be helpful would be some insights into—"

"Twyla, that's enough!" Lek glared at her until she let out her breath in silence. He glanced sharply at Mike. "All right. Let's just cool off. The purpose of this is to help each other, not tear each other down. Take a ten-minute break." He rose to his full six-foot height and motioned for everyone to get up and leave. As Twyla stalked off, Lek caught Mike's eye. "Let's go for a walk."

Mike gulped and followed Lek around to the far side of the ship. "I didn't mean to—" he began.

Lek waved him to silence. He took a deep breath and let it out slowly. He squinted up at the imposing form of the racing ship and gazed at her silently for a few moments. Mike waited nervously. "This craft," Lek said finally, "is a miracle of engineering, you know that? There's a lot of thought, a lot of genius, that's gone into making this ship. These racers fly like nothing else in the galaxy. They're amazing. Just amazing."

He lowered his gaze and shifted it to Mike. "You've been studying all that theory, Mike, all of those physical principles that go into making it work. You probably know more theory than any kid your age has ever known. I admire that."

Mike tipped his head ever so slightly in acknowledgment. He knew that Lek hadn't brought him over here to flatter him.

Lek's gaze wandered back to the ship. "But as

incredible as all that theory is, it's just a beginning. The pilot, the human half that flies the ship, is just as important as the technology. *More* important, because all the theory in the world can't make a good pilot." He brushed back his blond hair and squatted to examine the exhaust tubes beneath the ship. "I'm a scientific type myself, Mike. I'm not like Jass, say, who feels how to fly in his bones, like he was born for it. I have to work at the theory myself."

Mike knelt beside him, in puzzlement. "I know what you're saying," he said cautiously. "But how does that explain Twyla? Why did she get so mad, just because I?..." He let his voice trail off.

"That's the human half, Mike. The cussed half. The tough half to tame." Lek smiled briefly and got up. "Twyla's going to make a damn good pilot—you know that?"

"I know, but—"

Lek held up a hand again. "Mike, you were right. She was overcompensating. But she knew that already. She knows the theory as well as you or I. But there's a big difference between knowing the theory and carrying it out in practice. Now, it just so happens that the problem she was having is one that a lot of pilots have—it's one of the toughest things to teach, in fact. The simulations help, but there's just nothing like doing it for real. And it's *hard*. Even when you know the theory, even when you know what you're doing wrong—it's hard."

Mike frowned, gazing at his fingernails. He scratched his head and looked at the ship, avoiding Lek's eyes.

"So, what you didn't know, Mike, is that I was talking her through it, trying to help her get it right. And she's learning. But it can be awfully frustrating. So that's why she got mad. Even though you were right. You were both right."

Mike nodded and looked up. His eyes wandered about the pit and finally met Lek's gaze. He ran his fingers sheepishly through his hair. "Sorry," he croaked.

Lek smiled. "You might say that to Twyla, too. She'll forgive you. And hey—when you get a chance to fly, maybe you'll be lucky. Maybe that'll be a maneuver that comes naturally to you. But don't worry, you'll have some other weakness. We all have weaknesses."

Mike nodded. "Right."

"Now let's get back to the meeting, shall we?"

It was to be four days before the next series of training flights, and Mike had the opportunity to move about the pit crew, learning a bit here and a bit there about ship-tuning procedures. He stayed out of Twyla's way, but her anger had been short-lived in any case, and she'd accepted his apology with reasonable grace, though she hadn't gone quite so far as to offer one of her own.

In preparation for the next flights, Mike took over some of Andru's responsibilities for the tactical planning; Andru was busy working on some new schemes for later experimentation, and Mike was capable of handling the more established programming without Andru's help. Mike wasn't particularly worried about this, but he was mindful of the extra responsibility, and he tried doubly hard to get everything right the first time, and every time.

Perhaps he was trying *too* hard. How else to explain the error that slipped by him in the final readiness checks?

It would have been no big deal if it hadn't been for Twyla's error later. Mike had checked out the tactical programs the night before, disabling certain elements that would have interfered with the testing routines. After completing the tests, he somehow forgot to reenable one of the activation circuits.

The first he became aware of it was when Lek and Twyla were in their third lap, ready to practice a crossover maneuver—jumping from the passing lane on one side, *across* the groove, into the passing lane on the other side. The maneuver involved crossing two zones of velocity shear in rapid succession, and the purpose of the tactical program was to help smooth the jump. It was a tricky interaction of pilot and computer control; the program was supposed to assist the pilot without getting in the way.

Mike was following the progress on the monitor. He

heard Lek pass control to Twyla, with instructions to swing left—as though attempting to pass—then to jump suddenly right in response to an opponent's blocking maneuver. "Take it on my mark, Twyla," Lek said, his voice crackling back to the control shack. "I'll be controlling the ghost."

"I've got her," Twyla said.

On the screen, Mike could see the progress of the tactical programs as they ran. The setup was good; now the activation circuit should kick in when Twyla's steering command exceeded seventeen degrees right. He saw *her* mistake an instant before he saw his own.

"Passing left," Twyla sang. Her voice suddenly became taut, as Lek's ghost, the hypothetical opponent, veered momentarily out of the groove into the velocity shear, sending a wave of turbulence into her path. "Blocking," she muttered. "Cutting over . . ."

And on the screen, Mike saw her swing hard without first verifying the activation circuit—and in the same instant he saw that *he* had failed to enable the circuit. "You're not on—" he started to shout.

But she was already yelling, "It's bucking—*where the hell's the damper?*"

"You're not activated!" That was Lek's voice, barking.

"Damn it, why—?" Twyla's voice broke off, and on the screen were readings of racking turbulence, and Mike sensed Andru and the others wincing beside him as Twyla took the ship across both velocity shears without computer assist, and her voice stuttered from the console: "*Damn . . . damn . . . Lek, I can't hold it . . .*"

"I've got it, Twyla."

"*Damn . . . my arm . . .*"

"Hang on till I get her stabilized." Lek was trying to ease the ship through the last velocity shear into the passing zone, where things moved a little more slowly.

There was a lot of confusion as the pit crew tried to find out what was happening, but finally Lek's voice cut through. "Control, we're taking the next pit lane. This is *Slippery Cat* coming in. We got shaken up pretty hard. My copilot's hurt her arm, so we might need a medic rendezvous.''

Mike sat back, grim-faced. *Medic rendezvous?* He stared at the screens, hoping to see an answer that was different from the one he knew was going to come out of this. *I couldn't have left that off. I couldn't have done something that stupid. I couldn't have.* But he had. Whatever had just happened to Twyla . . .

''Mike, hey!'' It was Andru, gazing at him. ''You look like you just lost the fleet. Don't *worry,* Mike. She probably just got banged up a little when they hit that turbulence.''

Mike swallowed painfully and nodded.

''It's not that bad,'' Andru repeated softly.

''Yeah,'' Mike murmured.

It was a while before the *Cat* came back in, because Lek stopped first at the medical dock. By the time he'd gotten back to the pit, the clinic had already called with the news: Twyla had fractured a bone in her elbow, and she was going to be out for at least a few weeks, even with accelerated healing.

Mike barely listened, after the medical report. The other members of the crew were already speculating about what Lek would do to replace Twyla for the interim. Mike didn't want to hear about it. He busied himself stowing equipment, once the ship had been ''safed'' by the venting and sealing of dangerous chemicals. For a half-hour he barely looked up; then he was startled to feel a tap on his shoulder.

It was Lek. ''Come on, Mike—time for debriefing.'' Mike nodded, but without enthusiasm, and Lek added, tiredly, ''Aren't you being a little hard on yourself?''

Mike shrugged. He didn't try to hide his self-disgust. ''I don't know how I could have done it. I left that circuit off. But I *checked* it, Lek. I was *sure* I checked it.''

''So it was your fault that Twyla got hurt? Is that what you're saying?'' Lek asked.

''It's pretty obvious, isn't it?''

Lek glanced at him sharply. "Is it? I thought that was what the debriefing was supposed to tell us."

Mike fell in alongside him. "Yeah. But we already know. *I* do, anyway."

Lek stopped in his tracks and glared at him. "I'm glad *you* know, Mike—because *I* don't, yet." Lek cut off Mike's protest. "Okay, maybe you left the circuit off. Let's just say you did. Well, it had better not happen again. But aren't you forgetting something?"

Mike frowned.

"Twyla tried to use the circuit without checking it first," Lek said. "That was pilot error. Mike, you've got to learn that people sometimes make mistakes. People don't always work right, and equipment doesn't always work right—and that's why we always double-check one another!" Lek's eyes were penetrating. "So before you blame yourself altogether, remember: it may have been Twyla's fault as much as it was yours—and I think she knows that!"

Mike blinked, and stared at his boss. He frowned as the logic slowly soaked in.

"Now shall we go to the meeting?" Lek asked softly.

Mike nodded and followed, his footsteps a little lighter.

The meeting, to be sure, was a somber affair. The temporary loss of Twyla was a setback to Lek, throwing the racing schedule for the next several weeks into question; and the ship itself would have to be checked over carefully for damage. With a race coming up on the schedule in less than a week, the team would have to retrench, and fast, if there was to be any hope of competing. Analysis of flight telemetry confirmed that the accident resulted from a combination of Mike's error and Twyla's. Neither error alone would have caused a mishap, and it was fortunate that nothing more serious had happened. There was some discussion of how to prevent this sort of thing from happening in the future, but it mainly boiled down to everyone's being more careful. Soon the subject turned to finding a replacement for Twyla.

Lek rubbed his ear for a moment. "Well," he said, "we've got to have a relief pilot. But she's only going to be out for a couple of races, so instead of hiring a permanent replacement, maybe we've got someone on board already who could stand in for her." He glanced in Mike's direction. "Think you're up to doing a little flying, Mike? It won't be permanent, and—" he chuckled, "I don't think you'll be ready to fly in the Sam Adams, but . . ." He shrugged, and tugged at his earlobe. "What do the rest of you think?"

Mike's head swam as the others murmured their general approval. He tried to stutter out an answer. "Sure, but—but—"

"But what?"

"Well, I mean—after today? The way I blew it?"

Lek leaned forward and stared at him. "I thought we'd straightened that out already. So you blew it. So'd Twyla. You think I never blew anything? You think Andru never did?" He looked sideways and chuckled. "Well, maybe Andru didn't." After everyone laughed, at Andru's expense, Lek became serious again. "When you fall off a horse, you get back on. When you crack up a landing, you get right back in another craft—assuming someone will let you fly one." He grinned. "Well, I'm letting you fly one. Now, what do you say?"

Mike's face split in a smile. What *could* he say?

There was one duty he had to take care of that he would rather have avoided, and that was apologizing to Twyla. She was back at the docks the following day, with her arm in a rapid-healing cast, and she didn't smile when she saw Mike, but neither did she say anything.

Mike let a few minutes go by while he worked at one of the computer screens. Finally he took a deep breath and walked over to where she was sitting, studying the postflight telemetry printouts. He steeled himself and said, "Hi, Alley Cat."

Twyla looked up, startled. She was frowning. She looked as though she didn't recognize the name.

Mike cleared his throat. "How's the arm?"

She shrugged. "It'll be okay." Her voice was flat. Whatever she felt, she was keeping it to herself.

"Uh—well, I just wanted to say—"

"Just do a good job, okay?"

"Huh?"

"For Lek. For the team." She scowled down at the printouts for a moment, then said, "There were too many mistakes yesterday. Too damn many mistakes." There was a trace of bitterness in her voice.

"I know and I'm sorry about—"

"*Look,*" she said forcefully. "We both screwed up. Both of us, all right? But I was the pilot, so I was responsible."

"Okay," he answered softly.

"It's the team that counts." Twyla pressed her lips together as Mike nodded. "Don't get the idea that I'm taking this okay—because I'm not," she added. "I hate it. I hate this thing." She poked her cast with her left hand. "And it hurts like hell, if you want to know." She pursed her lips. "But it's the team that counts."

Mike cleared his throat uncomfortably. "Right."

"So just don't embarrass us."

"Right." He felt his face redden.

"Like I did," she added. She looked back at her printouts.

Mike nodded—more to himself than to her. He guessed that was the closest she would come to accepting his apology. He began to walk away.

"Hey, Junkyard," she said.

Mike turned.

She didn't look up as she growled, "Don't blame yourself."

Mike smiled faintly. "Right," he said and turned away.

CHAPTER 11

Race day was upon them before Mike had a chance to blink three times. Or so it seemed.

"Go for spin-up, *Slippery Cat*."

"Roger. Mike, you handle the tracking. Give me three ghosts and let's see how we can handle them."

"Ghosts away! This is *Cat*. We're in spin-up, transfactor one . . . accelerating to trans two . . . ."

"Ghost on your tail, Lek. Coming up in passing lane, eight o'clock."

"I see him, Mike. Let's give that shimmy program another try."

"Program running . . ."

"Get a little closer, spook . . . that's good . . . swerving now . . ."

"He's hitting turbulence, Lek. He's losing on us."

"Gooood. . . ."

"*Slippery Cat*, this is *Green Acres*. Care to go one-on-one? We promise not to hurt you."

"Ho-ho! You're on, Greenie. We promise not to spill your secrets to the rest of the competition."

"What secrets? There's no secret to skill, Lek!"

"We'll be watching. Mike, keep a close eye on this joker, until we leave him safely behind."

"Your *mother*, Lek. . . ."

132

* * *

"Thanks for the run, *Green Acres*."

"You won't get us next time, Croveen."

"Give the credit to my apprentice. You should teach *your* apprentice some racing theory. . . ."

"Theory? Give me a break!"

"Mike, looks like we're alone on this run. I want you to practice some jumps into passing lane. You looked good on the simulator yesterday. Game to try it for real?"

"Yow—are you kidding?"

"Hey, if you're not ready . . ."

"I'm *ready!* Just stay with me, Lek. Stay with me. . . ."

"Cut the chatter and go!"

"Go for spin-up, *Slippery*. Race starts on green."

"Roger. Mike—she's all yours."

"Say again?"

"Take her out. For the whole run. Let's see what you can do."

"Yowee! I mean, uh—taking her now."

This time was for real.

Twelve ships were gathered for entry into the warpweb, ready for the start of an AAA-class twenty-lap stock race. The clustered ships were moving slowly away from Pitfall, toward the grid that marked the entry belt in points of light. Pitfall's Race Control was murmuring in the ears of the pilots, coordinating the start.

Mike was sweating under the collar of his helmet. Beside him, Lek was cool and calm, ready.

"Gentlemen, test your engines!"

Lek hit the power switch and the ship reverberated with contained power. Mike studied the readings and gave Lek a go-ahead—as if Lek weren't watching every reading himself. The vibration faded away and Lek took the *Cat* outward under smooth acceleration. Eleven other ships soared out toward the equator in an expanding formation.

Each pilot would choose his or her own point to hit the entry belt. Where one hit didn't matter; all points were equidistant from the start of the racing web.

For Mike's first real race, he was going to keep his mouth shut and his eyes on the instruments—except when Lek asked for something, or he himself spotted something that Lek ought to know. Lek would be doing all the flying.

"Set, Mike?"

"Everything looks good."

"I meant *you*. Are *you* set?" Lek turned his head and gazed at him, a silver-visored creature from the stars.

Mike grinned back, his fingers itching in the control recesses of the console. He saw Lek through a ghostly pattern of readouts on his own visor. "Ready and rarin'. Ten seconds now . . . seven . . . six . . . ."

The drive kicked him in the rear.

When the ships leaped into the spin-up together, it was like a school of dolphins diving into the bow wave of a ship, darting and swarming for position. Twelve fusion drives blazed, lighting the screens with twelve identifying colors and the dancing silhouettes of the ships.

Mike was caught up at once in a flood of information from the tracking computer. He tried to sort out the changes while Lek jockeyed with the pack for position. One racer had gone out with exceptional power, risking his engines at the outset to capture the lead. Lek was on the opposite side of the pack at the time, and so it was two other ships that managed to capitalize on the leader's drag to take the second and third slots as they hit the main racing circle. Lek was doing well to slip into fourth, ahead of two other very good, aggressive racers. The rest were quickly strung out behind, in the groove. By the time Lek hollered for an update on who was where, Mike was locked into the computer output as though it were an extension of his own brain, which it very nearly was; his eye movements called up screen displays, his thoughts flowed with the data stream, and his fingers danced in the recesses of the control box.

He left his nervousness behind, somewhere near the plane of the ecliptic—and they were now climbing up over the solar north pole. He briefed Lek on the positions of the other racers, especially those following, which were harder for Lek to track himself—and he took an instant to glance at the wide-angle viewscreen. His breath caught again. The web shimmered, a ghostly golden spiderweb, and flowing along it were the glowing torches of the racers. Outside the web, almost at right angles around the sun now, was the almost invisible warp-tube system connecting the planets.

It was only a moment's look, but when his eyes and his thoughts flicked back to the instruments, he had to readjust quickly. Someone was in the passing lane behind them, gaining. "Lek . . ." he warned, and gave his partner the position.

Lek responded at once, swerving to create turbulence. The other racer dropped back. Lek lost a little distance, too, from the ship directly ahead of him. He grunted and immediately gave the *Cat* a short extra boost, to close again. He pushed the throttle back and forth a little, testing the other pilot's reactions. Mike watched carefully, and wondered if he was getting ready to attempt a pass.

He found out soon. "Mike, when we hit the g-beacon at six o'clock, we're going to run the chute and try to slip by Joe up here. Run a close herd on those engines and the tracking, and holler if there's anything that says I shouldn't go for it."

"I'm on it," Mike answered tightly, swallowing hard.

Running the chute was something he'd barely had a chance to practice—and it had only been added as an option to this race due to a late change in the web-circuit. Certain courses contained embedded gravity beacons; as the tube looped around the beacons, the racers could select among several difficult, high-speed bypass lanes that passed the beacons in tight slingshot configurations. As a faster way to get by a leader, the beacons were enticing—and tricky. They could put you out front or they could flatten you.

Mike wasn't experienced enough to risk it, but Lek was.

As they looped over the north pole of Clypsis, the ghostly interplanetary web seemed to tip toward them, then grow like a shimmering target. The two webs intersected cleanly, and as they dived, the glowing blips of the racers blinked one after another through the plane of the ecliptic; then they were racing toward the south pole of their orbit. Toward the beacon.

It looked like a kink in the web, an unraveling of the strand where the high-speed lanes twisted free and then rejoined the main path on the other side. It was coming up fast. Mike scanned the instruments, fine-tuned the engines, watched the other racers, murmured on the comm to Andru back in the pit, and kept his fingers crossed. "Looking good . . ."

"Pam's going for it, too," Lek muttered. "Fynck and Bev'n, in the number two—"

The second-position ship darted into one of the bypass lanes with a burst of light. There was no time to watch the outcome. The third ship held to the groove. "Still looks good," Mike said. Lek swerved. There was a flare-up in the screens, and they were in the chute.

Lek flew with grim concentration. Just maintaining control was trickier here. If he strayed even a little, he would lose speed rather than gain it; if he strayed too much, he could lose control of the ship. The beacon loomed just outside the webtube, glowing red and creating distortion lines in the tube itself; the bend was coming; Mike practically breathed numbers as he followed the tracking arrays; Lek steered tightly and cleanly . . .

There was a blaze of crimson light as they shot around the beacon, peaking at transfactor six, then drop ping back to trans four; the junction was coming up now, and they were going to beat the number-three ship, and Mike was watching the instruments like a hawk, there was a collision-avoidance system, but if it should fail. . . . There was another flare-up, and they were back in the main groove—*in the number-three position.*

"That's the way to fly!" Mike heard, and it was Andru, who'd seen it all on his monitors. But there was no time to respond, because Joe and Edie, the former number-three team, were on their tail, and Lek was gaining on number two, Jordan and Williams, who had been the leader. Fynck and Bev'n were now number one. And so it would stay for the moment, but only until the next opportunity to pass. . . .

It happened in the sixth lap.

Lek was still in third, and Jordan and Williams were taking great risks to recapture the lead position—swerving hard into the passing lane and back, and undoubtedly pushing their engines to the limit. Race Control had given them a yellow light already, warning of a violation of racing code. One more warning and they would be out of the race. They seemed undeterred, and Lek was having to fly conservatively just to stay out of their way.

In the end it was two other pilots who paid with them the cost of their recklessness. Jordan and Williams took the slingshot on the sixth lap—or tried to. Lek saw it coming and veered into the right bypass as Jordan and Williams shot left. Mike tracked the other ships carefully— Lek had to try either to hit the groove ahead of them or to fall in again behind—and Mike's heart jumped as he saw Jordan and Williams wobble a little in the chute and lose ground. Lek was flying well and true, and as they came out of the glowing close-approach, Mike sang out, "You've got the room—take it ahead of them!"

Lek complied without blinking, and they hit the groove in second position, close behind the leader.

Then the stern viewscreen flared and the board lit

up with alarms. Race Control's voice filled Mike's helmet:

"The red light is on! All drives off! Repeat—the red light is lit! All ships on maneuvering power only. . . ."

Lek killed the drives at once. They did not stop, or even slow, but continued in midstream through the web, coasting along with all the other ships in the stream of warped space circling the sun at three times the speed of light. But something had happened . . .

"Lek—" Mike said, his voice shaking a little. The data was being sorted out in the computer, and what it looked like was that one, and perhaps two, ships had disintegrated in the web. The groove—and most of the warptube—was strewn with debris.

"I see it," Lek said. "Andru," he called back to the pit, "did you pick up what happened?"

There was a hiss of static for a few moments, and then Andru's Merkek voice, unusually quiet: "Jordan and Williams lost control in the chute. They were tumbling when they hit the groove—and they came out right in front of Joe and Edie . . ." The distant voice hesitated, ran out of words. Then he seemed to catch his breath again. "The signals got scrambled all to hell, so we couldn't see what happened. But—"

"Thanks," Lek said. He turned his head to glance at Mike. Behind the silvered visor Mike could imagine Lek's eyes, sad and penetrating.

Then Race Control interrupted again:

"The double-red light is on! All ships to the pit lane! All ships return to Pitfall! The race has been terminated. . . ."

The official debriefing was conducted with the twenty surviving pilots and their top pit representatives. Twyla joined Lek and Mike; most of the backers were present, as well. The summary was brief enough: two ships and four pilots lost, the race called due to hazardous racing conditions, no purse awarded. Blame was tentatively attributed to pilot error. There was considerable anger among the pilots toward Jordan and Williams, who as far as most of the pilots were concerned had clearly caused the accident and taken two other, well-liked pilots with them when they punched into the sun. An official inquiry would be convened, but further racing would not be held up long. Accidents happened. All pilots knew it, and they accepted the risks, or they wouldn't be racing pilots. The racing community mourned its losses, but it carried on. As soon as the web was cleared, the racing—and the wagering—would resume.

Mike left the debriefing feeling stunned and depressed. He'd known, of course, that things like this were a possibility. But seeing it on the homescreen was different from having it happen in real life. And not just real life, but in his own race—just seconds from his own hide. Lek, for once, had nothing to say. Joe and Edie had been friends of his. Mike wondered if they were the first friends Lek had lost this way. He had a feeling not. But he wasn't going to ask, at least not right now.

Even Twyla was nearly silent. Perhaps this was, for her—as well as for Mike—the first close contact with death on the circuit. During the debriefing, Mike had seen tears running silently down her cheeks. Neither of them had spoken of it; but as they walked back, Mike for the first time felt some of the same comradeship with her that he felt for his other crewmates.

The others were waiting back at the pit. Lek held a short team debriefing to examine the flight crew's performance during the race. It was a joyless discussion, and after a few minutes he abruptly called it off. No one seemed to feel much like leaving, however. While Andru made a large pot of coffee, Dwaine disappeared and returned soon with all four arms laden with enough Siriun grilled pizza for the whole crew, and they all sat together in the pit office, eating and trying to talk racing, but with the conversations marked by a lot of pauses and unfinished sentences.

Finally, as the hour grew late, Lek disappeared to make some calls. He reappeared a few minutes later with two announcements. One was that a memorial service had been scheduled for the pilots who had died today. The other was that the next race on their docket was to be flown as previously scheduled. "That's in a week," he said to the crew, and he looked at Mike. "I didn't bring this up before, because I wanted you to have a race under your belt first."

Mike looked up slowly. Everyone was watching him—except Twyla, who was staring at the wall in apparent fascination. "What is it?" he asked.

Lek scratched his cheek thoughtfully. "The apprentices' race, of course. It was to have been Twyla's. But . . ." Lek pressed his lips together and glanced at Twyla sympathetically. "Since she won't be back on the active roster yet, our backers just approved my recommendation that you take her place."

Mike's mouth opened, and no words came out. The apprentices' A-class race. He'd known about it, of course. But it had been Twyla's, and he just hadn't thought . . . no one had said . . .

"You won't be flying the *Slippery Cat*. They'll be flying special ships—the academy's fleet, actually. They're a little tamer, and you'll be using circuit one, which is pretty straightforward. But you'll be flying solo." He paused for a moment. "I know, after today, maybe you don't feel like jumping right back onto the course. I wouldn't blame you. But if you're going to do it, we don't have much time left to prepare you. What do you say?"

Mike stared at the floor for a moment, mind reeling. At the moment, it was hard to imagine climbing into a racer and flying. But how was he going to feel tomorrow? What would Speedball Raybo say if he were here? He glanced up to see Twyla frowning, tugging at her hair with her good hand. Mike hesitated, wondering if she would regard this as the ultimate theft of her position . . . or as his chance to prove himself worthy of standing in for her.

"Mike?"

Twyla's frown deepened, and as their eyes finally

met, Mike realized that she was moving her head in an almost imperceptible nod. He looked up at Lek. "Okay," he said in a whisper. "Yes, of course." He took a breath. "Start tomorrow?"

Lek nodded. "Tomorrow."

Putting the disaster behind them was no easy matter. Mike almost lost his nerve during the memorial service for the fallen pilots. But as quickly as the doubts crowded in upon him, a new breath of courage welled up from somewhere deep inside him, and he resolved to fly this first solo race for the memory of a couple of pilots he had never known.

He hurled himself into preparing for the race, spending hours in the simulator with programs to emulate the less-powerful ship he would be flying against his fellow apprentices. Twyla had her own work to do, getting ready for her return to flight status; nevertheless, she worked diligently in the simulator with Mike, trying to make him fly harder and faster, especially in the areas where he was weakest.

There was a noticeable change in Twyla's attitude, which made Mike wonder if she had been affected even more than he by the deaths of the pilots. She was a little less impatient and short-tempered, and when she did flare up, she no longer directed her wrath personally at him, at least not in the same way. For the first time, she seemed genuinely interested in helping him. As he suited up for his first solo run in one of the academy ships, she remarked, "You've got to win this for me, Junkyard. If you win, then they'll *know* that I'm the best, since obviously I could fly rings around you." Mike grinned and gave her a thumbs-up. But beneath the joke, he sensed an earnestness that he'd never seen in her before.

He flew six times around the course that day, testing his skills in the student racer. It *was* tame compared to Lek's ship, but he felt freer in putting it through its paces and testing its limits more vigorously. And the entire pit crew, including Lek and Twyla, were on the comm circuit, coaching and encouraging him. By the time he returned to the pit, he was feeling jolly, confident, and ready.

Two days later he flew again, in final rehearsal. Though he flew well, he was now confident enough to analyze what he could do well and what he couldn't. It was a more humbling flight. But, he reminded himself, this was a race for apprentices. No one was expected to be a Lek Croveen—or a Speedball Raybo.

Tomorrow was race day.

"Checklist complete, Mike. Are you ready?"

Mike scanned the instruments one more time, before answering Andru. "*Junkyard*, aye. Ready to go."

"Moving you out, then. Give 'em hell."

"Roger." Mike moved out of dock. He felt the engine throb as he put it through the preflight test. Dwaine had checked the engine for him under the jealous eye of the academy mechanics and pronounced it fit. It felt good, and it looked good on the readouts.

Race Control was filling his ear with announcements, and on command he headed for the entry ring, flanked by eight others. He had a moment of quiet to reflect on what was to come, and to feel a stirring of fresh nervousness— and then the order came to fly into the spin-up ring, and the green light blazed.

The race was on.

Junkyard Dog shot into the web and hit the groove in third position, behind the two top-rated apprentices. Mike's head buzzed with excitement for a moment before the pressure settled in, the pressure of keeping his position, as well as of looking for an opportunity to move up. Behind him, six ships were in aggressive pursuit. In his headset, Andru and Lek were talking him on, but he hardly had time to listen, much less reply. Ahead of him, the torches of the two leaders flared in the web, but there was no time to enjoy the view. He had to fly with his whole mind and body, his entire *being* devoted to reflex action.

Fly tight. Fly right.

The ship behind him swung to pass, and he shimmied and threw turbulence into the fellow's path.

Hang tough.

The pursuer dropped back. The ship ahead of him fluttered its drive off and on, which put turbulence in *Mike's* path. The string of ships stretched out, Mike losing a little ground on those in front and gaining a bit on those behind. Two ships following him traded position, fifth for fourth. Mike throttled up, eyeing the pursuer as he strove to stay cleanly in the groove.

Don't screw up.

It was a dance, a kinesthetic movement, balancing the inflow of sensory and cybernetic data with the movement of the ship, balancing caution and daring, threading *himself* through the web and taking the ship along with him. The laps passed almost as though by magic, as though someone other than he were piloting; his subconscious was in control, the primitive reptilian remnant of his brain raising its head to control the slipping and the scooting and dodging for safety when a pursuer loomed close behind. There was a dim, distant sensation of revolving, whirling round and round the sun . . . *round and round and round she goes, where she'll stop, nobody knows!* . . . and the two leaders, both more experienced than he, eating up the miles and drawing away from him despite his efforts, the leaders nipping and tucking with one another while he, determinedly following but not quite keeping up, outpaced his predators from behind.

Time seemed to slip into another mode, quickening and slowing at once. The seconds stretched to minutes as course adjustments flowed through his fingertips, as he swung out of the groove to prevent a pass, swung tightly back in and kicked the throttle up to pick up speed again. But the minutes fled, as lap passed after lap, after lap . . .

He was stunned to hear Andru's voice shouting: "Are you listening to me, Mike? Do you hear me?"

How long had Andru been trying to get his attention? "Say again?" Mike said, not taking his attention from the array of tacticals . . . number four was maneuvering to try to pass again.

"Last lap, Mike! It's now or never! You're flying fine, but if you play cautious you're gonna lose it. Put it down, Mike, put it down. You've got the reserves. Lay a little smoke for us!"

Mike blinked, losing his edge for an instant. Playing cautious . . . had he been playing cautious? Was he holding back, was he afraid to put it on the line? The image of the accident flickered through his mind, and he savagely suppressed it. "Yeah, I copy you, pit . . ."

"Hit the needle, *Junkyard!*" Twyla called. "You're out of time! Redline it!"

Right . . . redline it . . . *now!*

He kicked to full thrust.

And it happened so fast he scarcely saw it: the ship behind him was in the passing lane and really *flying,* and the guy was around him before he could do more than blink . . . *damn it, you idiot!*

"Mike, stay with it! Don't let him get away!" Andru cried.

Mike swung hard into the passing lane an instant after the other cut in front of him. He had the reserves left, and the other had just used his, but Mike was redlining even as he drew close alongside . . .

"Last point, last lap, Mike!"

There were only seconds left in the race. The two leaders flashed across the finish, one after another. Mike and his foe were dancing side by side, the disk of the ecliptic looming . . . The other racer shimmied to slow Mike, but Mike swung down and below him, missing the turbulence, and the power the other lost in that instant *might* just have made the difference . . . and Mike drew even as they screamed toward the plane of the ecliptic and the finish . . . *and he had it, he had it, he had it!*

The white light strobed on his board as the ecliptic flashed by, and he heard the cry: *"Finish!"* and he let out a long breath and eased his engine back and listened for the good news:

"*Tying for third, Mike Murray in* Junkyard Dog *and Randall Grrrs'n in . . .*"

Stunned, he listened again. *Tied for third? No! . . .*

He barely heard the rest as he swung into the pit lane. He was *sure* he had passed the guy. How could they say it was a tie? Lek and Andru and Twyla were calling congratulations to him, and yeah, he had placed—but he'd come *so close* to doing better!

In a voice filled with melancholy, he called, "*Junkyard Dog*, coming in . . . ."

CHAPTER 12

"**W**ell, I guess I'd feel better if I hadn't blown it at the end. I *had* that guy, Jass, I *had* him."

Jass shook his head, chuckling. "Mike, you idiot—don't you know you weren't even supposed to have a *prayer* of placing in that race? Didn't Lek talk to you?"

"Well, yeah—he tried to cheer me up." Mike ran his fingers through his hair with a sigh. "They all did. They said I did okay." He glanced up at the pedestal-stage, where the musicians were returning. Why didn't he feel like he'd done okay?

"Cheer you up?" Jass sat back and grinned. "I don't think *they* needed any cheering up, Mike. They thought you did great. Get used to it. You don't win every race. Even Speedball didn't do that."

Mike nodded, watching the musicians. Several of them were Merkeks, but the lead singer was Arcturan, an exotic, dark-haired, triple-breasted female named Darney Quebble. He knew Jass was right—Lek had said much the same thing after the race—but he just couldn't shake the feeling that he *should* have done better. He laughed suddenly and turned back to his friend. "Didn't Speedball feel bad when he lost? Didn't you?"

Jass cocked his head and grinned. "Touché"

The Arcturan singer was rising in the center of the stage now to thunderous applause. The music beat across the room: ". . .Sometimes I get kind of crazy, crazy. . . ."

Mike sighed as the music flowed through him. But as

146

he listened, he felt his mood slowly begin to lift, and he thought: he had done pretty well for himself, hadn't he? After all?

Hadn't he?

"Mike, I hate like hell to do this to you, after the terrific showing you gave the other day," Lek said, "but Twyla's just been cleared by the medics for flight status. I guess you know what that means."

Mike nodded unhappily. At least Lek had waited to tell him, had given him a couple of days to bask in the pleasure of his status. There was a terrible irony in having to relinquish his spot now, of all times—but he'd known that it was coming. It gave him some idea of how Twyla must have felt when she'd had to step aside. Now it was his turn to do likewise, as graciously as he could manage.

"Don't worry, Mike," said another voice. "You'll fly again."

Mike turned in surprise. Twyla had walked up behind him, unnoticed. She was gazing at him steadily, somberly. Slowly a smile creased her lips, and she put out her hand. Mike took it, and she gripped it firmly. "I, uh—I guess you're the new old apprentice pilot," he said, trying to keep his voice steady.

She nodded. "You'll be flying again," she repeated. "Probably won't be as long as you think. A lot of people saw how well you did the other day."

Mike shrugged uneasily. "I suppose . . ."

"I might not have made it clear before," Twyla said. She cleared her throat awkwardly. "I mean—that I'm sorry I was being such a creep."

"Well—you weren't—"

"I wasn't putting the team first. That's right." Twyla hooked her thumb at Lek, who was watching the two with interest. "Even Lek, here, puts the team first. Isn't that right, Lek?" The pilot smiled, and she gazed into space, nodding. "I kind of got to thinking about it, after—well, you know. The accident. Anyway, from now on . . ."

Mike allowed the corner of his mouth to curl up in a one-sided grin. "Right," he finished. "Team first."

"I say," Lek said. "Don't we all have work to do? Big race in a few weeks, and all that?"

"Aye, Captain," said Twyla, saluting.

Mike echoed the salute.

Lek raised his eyebrows and turned away, trying to hide a grin.

Mike wouldn't have thought it possible, but for the next three weeks he worked murderously hard—harder even than in preparation for his own race. He'd known it was coming, of course, but recent events had practically driven it from his mind. This was the Three-Star Samuel Adams Premium race—widely known as the Sam—an annual spectacle that was considered *the* event for racers of Lek's class. It was almost as big an event as the Five Star classics; the ships were nearly as fast, and it was a race in which future Five Star winners often emerged into the public eye. Just running in the race conferred considerable prestige, and the winner would walk off with a hefty prize. If Lek and Twyla put in a good showing, it would mean greater interest from backers and a more secure future for the team as a whole.

The team, in fact, was pulling together as never before. Mike hadn't been aware of it, but the tension that had existed earlier between Twyla and him had affected everyone—not severely, perhaps, but enough to create minor stresses, ripples of irritation that had kept the crew from doing their best work. Now they were working together smoothly, and though they were all working exceptionally long hours, no one minded. There would be time to relax later. Right now, excitement was building with the approach of the race.

Mike cancelled two dinners in a row with Jass, and finally called him and asked sheepishly if it would be all right if they got together *after* the race.

Though there was hardly any aspect of the preparation that Mike didn't assist in, most of his energy went, with

Andru's, into refining the tactical programming. There were several computer-aided maneuvers that still didn't work quite as Lek wished, and for four days Mike ate, slept, and breathed tactical maneuvers. He and Twyla tested them in the simulator every chance they had, and once they were satisfied, they gave the program to Lek to test, and he came back and said to go make it better.

They went back and made it better.

When Mike couldn't see straight at the computer anymore, he held tools and meters for Dwaine, who had practically become an extension of the *Slippery Cat*'s engines. With Twyla, he spent additional hours in the simulator, going one-on-one, with the expressed purpose of sharpening Twyla's skills, but honing his own, as well.

As race day approached, Mike didn't see how they could possibly be more prepared. Lek assured him that there were *always* ways to be more prepared, and pointed out some new deficiencies in the programming. Mike grunted and went back to work. An hour later, he realized that there was no way he could possibly have all the bugs out in time for the race. All he could do was try, and he poured himself into the programming. . . .

Race day.

Someone had strung up a banner that read: LEK CROVEEN: FUTURE CHAMPION! The crew, most of them, had arrived hours early, and when Lek himself strode in, they gave a rousing cheer. Lek laughed and thanked them, not without some embarrassment, and quietly asked them to take down the banner. "Just until after the race," he said. "I'm not a champion yet, so let's not jinx us before it happens, okay?"

Mike spent the hours before rollout making last-minute checks on the tacticals. He drank too much coffee and stared at the screens until his eyes blurred, and by rollout, he'd convinced himself that the programming was a complete loss, that there was just no way it could work. How was he going to tell Lek and Twyla? They ought to just keep it turned off.

He felt a bony hand on his shoulder. "How much more can you check it?" Andru said with a dry chuckle. "Time to upload it. Lek needs to give it a run-through in about fifteen minutes."

"But—"

"It'll *work*, Mike. Quit worrying."

Mike sighed and slapped his thighs. "Okay."

The Racing Commission monitors were filled with images and talk of the race; there was already a preliminary AA-class race under way, and betting for the Sam was reaching a high pitch. As Mike paused on his way out of the office to peer at the public coverage on the monitor, he wondered—were the investors holding their breaths, or was this just another day in the life for them? He flicked the channel and found a bulletin-board message addressed to Lek and the crew. It was from the Frank L. James syndicate, wishing them success; Mike flicked again, and found a message from Jass Blando, telling them to go for the big number one.

"Mike, I need you!"

He grinned and hurried out. Lek was standing in the hatchway of *Slippery Cat*, cupping his hand to shout again. Mike trotted over. "Twyla's having problems with the computer. See if you can help her," Lek snapped, hooking his thumb inside. He looked upset.

Mike ducked through and found Twyla muttering furiously over the consoles. Mike slipped into the other seat. "What's not working?"

"The damn programs aren't running!"

Mike's blood went cold. "None of them? What do the diagnostics say?" He donned a helmet, slipped his hands into the control recesses.

"Tacticals only, damn it." Twyla snapped several overhead switches. "We've got a failure mode in unit three, but it won't isolate."

"Can't we just swap it out?"

"Haven't got a bloody damn replacement. I *told* Andru we should have something on hand . . ."

Mike groaned. After all that work, and an hour before the race!

"I *told* him—"

"He can't have a spare for every single part," Mike said softly. "That's supposed to be a high-reliability module—"

Twyla snorted and got up out of her seat. "I have to talk to Lek."

Nodding, Mike began running the diagnostics again. There had to be something he could do. . . .

He'd found no solution when Lek appeared, his tall frame filling the cramped cockpit. "Are we going to have to go without it?" Lek asked.

Mike scowled and nodded slowly, his teeth almost puncturing his lower lip. "Yah. I'll keep working—"

"Can you program around it?"

Mike felt the pressure building on the inside of his forehead. "I'll try," he whispered.

Lek's face was creased with worry as he took Mike's place in the pilot's seat. Mike knew that Lek could fly without the tacticals if he had to; but against the best pilots of his class, all with computer-assist, it would surely be a losing battle.

Mike dashed back to the control shack, yelling for Andru.

There had to be a way. . . .

By rollout time, they had discovered the failure mode of the component and were trying to find a way around it. Mike's heart missed a beat as he heard the call for ships to leave dock and test their engines. Lek's voice filled the shack as he reported readiness, though they all knew he couldn't really be ready unless a solution was found.

Andru had to leave Mike to it while he dealt with more immediate problems—and Mike felt a shiver run through his body as he struggled to merge his thoughts with the computer routines, seeking an answer. *There had to be a way!* The announcement, *"On the green light . . ."* was a distant echo in his ears, but at the back of his consciousness, he saw the light flash.

The race was on, and he couldn't even take a moment to glance, to see it happening . . .

"Fly her, Lek, fly her!" he heard someone cry. And he knew Lek was a good flyer, but could he possibly be that good?

"Fourth position, slipping to fifth. . . ."

The program streams glowed in Mike's mind like a tangled three-dimensional roadmap . . . he probed . . . tested . . . if he could wall off certain actions and alter the sequences of others . . . he was certain now that there was a way to do this, but it would take days to find it, to test it . . . he didn't have days, he only had minutes . . .

The laps passed, and in the back of his head, he heard Twyla's voice reporting and Andru's suggesting, and he heard the grim determination in Lek's as he flew by the seat of his pants and held his own, but without the incredible precision he needed to get by those ahead of him. He heard Twyla asking, "Has Mike found anything yet?" and he couldn't answer, but he heard Andru answering, "Not yet, still working . . ."

Damn it, there *had* to be . . .

Lap five, moving into lap six.

And the answer began to materialize . . . first a tickle in the forebrain, then with a great swelling in Mike's chest as he saw the connections . . . for a moment he could not breathe as he made the alterations and tested them, then his breath exploded in a shout, "I've got it!" that brought Andru immediately to his side.

"Are you sure?" the Merkek demanded, watching the test on the screen.

"Let me double-check," Mike breathed. "But get Twyla ready to copy some changes fast."

The changes flickered, and the new paths lighted, and the answer was ambiguous; it looked like it *should* work, but would it work in all cases? He couldn't be sure.

"Twyla . . ."

"Yeah, we're a little busy here—"

"It's Mike. I think I've got it. Can you download?"

"Junkyard, I hope you know what you're doing . . . ."

Mike came up for air and took in the situation at a glance. Lek was still in fifth position, and the race was half over. The ships were strung out along the web, the leaders now darting past the gravity beacon and around the south pole of Clypsis and up. Lek had a lot of distance to make up, even if everything worked. But he'd been flying conservatively, saving fuel, saving his engines, holding his own but keeping his reserves for the end, just in case.

Twyla shouted, "Andru, we're not getting a clear signal!"

Andru's bony fingers flew. "Try it again!"

"Okay, it's loading . . ."

Mike clutched the edge of the console as he waited. *Please, please, please work . . .*

"It's loaded. Testing now . . ." Twyla's voice was calmer. "It seems to be working."

The next voice they heard was Lek's: "Jumping to pass—he's blocking—cutting back across *now*—and hard on the main!"

Mike peered at the screen and saw Lek's blip slowly passing the ship in fourth place. It shifted back into the groove and began gaining on the ship in third. "Is it working?" Mike whispered.

"Clean jump," Lek reported. "Mike, it looks good. Next time around we're taking the chute."

He was picking up ground again, but it was obvious that the only conceivable way to gain that much distance in the remaining time was to hit the chute hard and hit it clean—and do it every time from now to the end of the race. Most pilots wouldn't dare to try it so many times in a row—it was nerve-wracking and exhausting—but there was a new life in Lek's voice now, and if anyone had the stamina to try it, he did.

Keep working, just keep working, Mike prayed. While the ships rounded the sun in lap seven, Mike tested and retested his changes. He knew it wasn't foolproof, but if he could just find any other place it might fail, and warn them . . .

The images swelled again in his mind, the crisscrossing patterns of code . . .

A shout from one of the crew brought him back to the present as the ships swung through the north-pole loop and past another beacon. Lek hit the chute with full power and swept so close to the beacon that Mike's stomach dropped, watching from a billion kilometers away. He glared at the screen, watched the lineup reassemble as Lek and one other pilot aimed for the groove again—and there was a blaze of light as he came out of the chute—*and he was in third place.*

"By damn, Michael, when you fix something, you fix it!" Lek roared, his voice a crackle against the cheers of the crew.

"I try, Lek, I try," Mike breathed, not into the comm but to himself. It worked once . . . would it keep working? He turned his attention back . . . searching, testing.

For the next lap, it was Dwaine on the comm, telling Twyla to make almost infinitesmal changes to the engine fields, changes so trifling that only Dwaine would know that it would save the fields a little, give them a little more power, use a little less fuel. Then Andru was reporting to Lek on the patterns the two leaders had been following, where their weaknesses might be, where Lek might have a chance to pull past them. And Mike kept searching, with a gnawing suspicion that something was still not quite right.

Lek took the chute next time around, not to pass but to make up distance. He did it cleanly again, but not quite so cleanly. He was gaining on number two, but the front-runner had taken the slingshot, too, and was pulling away from its nearest pursuer. It looked to be virtually impossible for Lek to catch up with the front-runner, but as he reported back, his voice was as calm and cheerful as if he were chatting over coffee—except that beneath the calm there was an edge of determination.

And in the back of Mike's mind something snagged— and he quickly checked a slightly different scenario against the program . . .

The next time past the beacon, the leader stayed in

the groove; and Lek was gaining on number two, just close enough to make the try . . .

"Tell him not to go!" Mike screamed.

"Lek, don't go!" Andru snapped.

Lek obeyed, but a moment later said, "Mike—what the hell?"

Mike showed Andru on the screen as he explained it to Lek. At certain distances and angles, the failure mode reappeared. If Lek had taken the chute, he would have lost the tacticals in the moment of entry; and it was anyone's guess if he would have survived the passage unaided. They all remembered Jordan and Williams. Lek passed control of the ship off to Twyla while he listened, questioning Mike closely. "All right," he said finally. "You give me the go or the no-go, each time around. We'll be counting on you."

"Right." Mike swallowed his fear and kept searching.

The next time around, he gave Lek a "go"—and Lek took the chute, but so did the number-two ship. He didn't get by, but both of them gained on the number one, who held to the groove.

The time after, he gave Lek a "no-go." *There must be a solution to this, too. If he's to have any chance at all. . . .*

On the fourth-to-the-last orbit, Lek made a slingshot approach so close that it would have taken five years off Mike's life. He nearly overloaded his engines—but the fine-tuning made the difference, and he captured the number-two slot. The control room went wild.

Except Mike. He knew that Lek needed to repeat that performance three more times, or it would all be for nothing. And Mike still didn't have a handle on this thing . . .

He almost didn't hear Lek calling for a go/no-go the next time around, so immersed was he in the program; but he came to suddenly and called "Go!" and watched in horror as the computer failed again, at the very end of the slingshot, and only through sheer skill did Lek hold his course firm. He picked up a little distance on the leader, but lost a little on the ship he'd just passed, which was now breathing down his neck. For Mike, it was this lap or none at all; with that last failure, the whole program had shut down, and Twyla reported full failure mode.

Mike felt himself panicking. But a pattern was beginning to emerge, and he forced himself to breathe and to focus . . . and when the pattern finally took shape in his mind, it was like a time-lapse holo of a crystal growing, and *there it was*, the flaw in the programming, as clear as it could possibly be: a subroutine that sent conflicting signals to the inertial guidance, setting up a cascading chain that caused the entire routine to fail. Now that he saw it, he wondered in astonishment: Why hadn't he seen it before? *And there was no hardware failure at all—it was a problem in the loading routine of the program!* And as the image grew in his mind, so did the solution. But was there time to do anything about it?

Andru was on the horn talking strategy with Lek and Twyla: ". . .you're going to have to redline the last lap . . . Dwaine says she thinks you can make it hold if you—"

"Andru!"

"Hold it, Lek." The tactician shifted his gaze. "What?"

"I've got a solution! Tell Twyla to get ready to reload! It's not the computer, it's the—"

"Don't explain, just do it," Andru snapped. "Twyla, we've got a change for you to download!"

"Are you kidding?" Twyla said through a burst of static. "We don't have time for that now!"

"You don't have time *not* to. Mike's got a solution. Lek, can you go off-line for a few seconds?"

Weariness was audible in the pilot's voice. Going off-line meant working even harder. "If you've got a solution, if you want me to, I'll dust off the sun." There was a pause, then: "We're off-line, go ahead."

Mike sent the coding in a burst.

It took about six seconds, plus ten more for verification. During that time, Lek struggled to fend off two passing attempts by the third-place ship. The chute was coming up, and there was no time to test, only to go. . . .

"Mike, are you *sure* about this?"

Mike hesitated only an instant. "As sure as I can be."

"Copy. We're going in."

The entire pit crew stared open-mouthed at the monitors as the *Slippery Cat* dived into the chute. Mike half-watched the computer output, half-watched the view from Lek's nose-camera. The computer was running . . . Lek was steering tightly and cleanly, and the assist was working perfectly . . . but the ship behind him had taken the chute on the other side, aiming for a pass . . .

Twyla's voice droned the information: ". . . transfactor six, six point five . . . hell of a tight angle, Lek . . ."

The mass beacon swelled, a glowing blood-red ghost in the twisting warpweb, and Lek surely had a deathwish, because he was taking it closer than ever, and the stress alarms were flashing . . .

The third-place ship was cutting it damn close, too; he seemed determined to get by . . .

. . . and the beacon yawned to swallow them in its shimmering unreality, and Twyla was calling out, ". . . transfactor seven!" and Lek redlined the engines, and the viewscreen went blue with radiation, and Twyla cried out in alarm . . .

The beacon vanished and they whipped out of the slingshot at *transfactor eight point five*, probably a course record, and when they hit the groove again they slowed, but they were still *screaming*, and the third-placer was fading away behind them now, and the lead ship was visible out front for the first time, its exhaust flaring violet. And Lek was gaining on him.

They flashed through the ecliptic, under the Dragon's Claw, and now they were in the final lap. Lek continued gaining—and now it was Lek and Dwaine and Twyla, tuning and retuning for the maximum conceivable output—and the leading pilot and crew must have been doing the same, because Lek began to close more slowly. But he was beginning to pick up the other ship's exhaust, and that meant a shade more power with a shade less fuel consumption as his intake gobbled the exhaust, and he began to close the gap more quickly again.

By the time they approached the chute one last time, Lek was hard on the other racer's tail, and Mike's heart was thundering as fast as the ship's engines. The public announcers were shouting a byplay, bordering on hysteria, and the pit crew were hopping and moaning and beating on one another, Andru and Dwaine alone keeping their voices calm enough to talk to Lek—mostly in monosyllables, leaving Lek free to fly and do nothing but fly.

The two ships hit the chute practically at the same instant, one to each side. Lek flew beautifully, but so did the other pilot—and the beacon loomed, blazing, and vanished, and they flashed back out into the groove—

—*and Lek was still in second place!*

Mike nearly screamed in despair, but Andru barked for quiet, and Dwaine snapped out one last tune-up instruction.

And Lek swung sharply and redlined deep into the danger zone—and Mike's heart nearly stopped, but Dwaine was watching every feedback, and she murmured her encouragement, "You can hold it, Lek, just a little longer, I'm watching it . . ."

It's going to blow, dammit, it's going to blow!

The ecliptic swung toward them, and the Dragon's Claw twisted across their path as Lek pulled even and pushed his engines a few ergs harder . . . they flashed through the ecliptic and the finish line, and the whole damn crew was shouting so much, Mike couldn't hear the official announcer, but he was praying his thanks because it *hadn't blown* and Lek was throttling back now, bringing the engines back, saving the coils. . . .

"Would everyone *please shut the hell up?*" Andru shouted, and the yelling tapered off a few decibels, and then Mike heard the announcers bellowing over and over:

"*. . .winning in a tremendous finish, an unbelievable finish, Lek Croveen and Twyla Rogres!*"

CHAPTER 13

By the time *Slippery Cat* was back in its dock, the pit area was hip-deep in racing officials, media, security people, spectators who'd gotten past the security people, and friends and well-wishers. Jass was there, the investors were there, several unidentified automatons were there, and so were an alien or two in atmosphere suits. It was all the pit crew could do to get the ship safely berthed.

Lek and Twyla stepped out to a tremendous cheer. Lek tried to get his pit crew around him for the cameras, but the racing officials drew the pilots away for on-camera interviews and for the presentation of medals and prize money. Mike and the others whooped and grinned and congratulated one another as they watched their boss on the monitors. Someone remembered the banner and they strung it up again.

Elsewhere, no doubt, the bettors of Pitfall were laughing and crying as they toted up their earnings and losses from another day of racing, an extraordinary day of racing on the Clypsis circuit.

When the media and crowds finally left—hours later, it seemed—the pilots and crew and a few friends finally adjourned to a favorite local watering hole for a private and enthusiastic celebration.

The party went on deep into the night.

"Speedball, I don't know how you find these people, but I have to hand it to you . . ."

Raybo's energy field shimmered up and down as he laughed. "You liked the way they pulled it out?"

"*Like* it? I was astonished," said Curtis Rochards, countering Raybo's last move with a diagonal jump-check in the 5-D playing field. Rochards inhabited a taller, slimmer psyche-vehicle than Speedball, with a darker energy field. He looked no more like a Rykell than Speedball looked like a human. "I knew they were talented. But there was no way Croveen was going to make that comeback, whiz kid on his team or not! Just no way—no matter how good a pilot he was. Two of his investors called halfway through the race to yell at me for recommending a loser—and I sympathized with them. I must learn to contain my doubts."

MIDNITE chuckled and executed a four-color cross, making the board image light up. MIDNITE was inhabiting one of his temporary PVs, a boxy crosshatched model with six arms. "I trust they're happier now."

"I should say so. They're talking about doubling their investment. But there are going to be a lot of people suddenly taking an interest in Lek Croveen. He'll be able to pick and choose, all right—but there are a lot of vultures out there."

"Lek's been around enough to take care of himself," Speedball said, pondering his next move. "It's young Murray I'm concerned about. He could be getting a lot of offers. And as you say, there are vultures."

"I'm sure we'll be able to help him," Curtis said. "But what's this I heard about your Earth police looking for him?"

"*What?*" Speedball cried.

"I'm looking into that now," MIDNITE answered. "I don't know how you heard about it so soon, Curtis. Do you hear *everything* that comes in here?"

"Well . . ." Curtis let his field flicker negligently. "I have my sources."

Raybo interrupted. "What are you two talking about? What police?" Damned cocky Rykell, he thought with a mixture of amusement and annoyance. Just like him to hold out on something like that. He was worse now than when he'd been alive.

"We just received a subspace inquiry from Earth authorities," MIDNITE said. "It seems Mike left home rather hurriedly—after a death in his family."

"What?" Curtis yelled.

MIDNITE laughed. "So you didn't hear everything. That's reassuring." He continued smoothly, "No, he wasn't responsible for the death if that's what you're worried about. But the police were trying to find him, nevertheless. It took them a while to trace him here—but it's connected to an inheritance, and not to any criminal matter."

Speedball was relieved. "So there's no problem."

"Well, I doubt that he can collect his inheritance until he's older, or has a legal guardian." MIDNITE paused a moment, then asked teasingly, "Interested?"

Raybo laughed. "I prefer to work behind the scenes. You know that."

"But you would qualify, probably—"

"That zombie?" Curtis interjected. "He's *dead*."

Raybo would have raised an eyebrow if he'd had eyebrows to raise. "Is the pot, pray tell, calling the kettle black?"

"Not black. Dead."

"Gentlebeings," MIDNITE interrupted, "this is, after all, a special case. Speedball has already practically adopted the boy."

"Now, wait a minute . . ." Raybo protested.

Curtis laughed.

Raybo hmm'd. He started to make a move on the board, then reconsidered. "You're serious, aren't you? I'll think about it. Right now I just want to make sure he doesn't do anything stupid."

"Understood. You don't have to decide now."

"Thanks." Raybo finally made his move—taking out four of his opponents' pieces.

"Anytime," said MIDNITE.

"You Earth-dog," said Curtis, eyeing the board ruefully.

"Hey, Junkyard!"

Mike turned. Twyla was coming out of the pit office, followed by Lek. They were both smiling—which was hardly surprising, considering what they'd won, two days ago. "Yo," he said.

"Got something to tell you," Lek said. "Or ask you, anyway."

"Sure. What?" Mike's own spirits were a little subdued. Maybe it was postflight letdown, after all the celebrating. Or maybe it was beginning to sink in that *they'd* won the fame and fortune, and he hadn't. He hated to admit it, but that bothered him a little.

"Come on in the office."

Mike followed them, wondering if they were finally going to grill him about the original screwup in the computer that had put them all through such turmoil in the race. It really hadn't been his fault, he wanted to say, at least not totally. But wait—they were smiling.

"Mike, sit down," Lek said.

Mike sat.

Twyla was perched on the edge of Lek's desk, looking at him with a mysterious frown. Lek offered Mike a cup of coffee. He accepted it and took a sip.

"So," Lek said.

"So," Twyla echoed.

Mike choked on his coffee. "So?" he croaked.

"Right. Twyla and I have been talking."

Mike looked at Twyla, and back at Lek. "Yeah?"

Lek shrugged. "Well, we just won a first-prize purse, you know, which is a good bundle of money—and on top of that, we've been getting inquiries galore from investors." Lek's eyes danced. "It seems that we're going to be disgustingly wealthy—at least for a little while—even after we pay all you guys your bonuses."

Mike raised his eyebrows. *Bonuses?* No one had told him about bonuses.

"So, anyway, we've been trying to think how we could spend some of that loot. And Twyla and I came up with an idea which we thought we ought to run past you."

"Uh-huh." Bonuses—this he liked.

"You tell him, Twyla," Lek said casually.

Mike shifted his gaze to meet her green-gold eyes. Twyla was grinning now. She scratched her ear and said, "So, Junkyard Dog, we're planning to add another ship to our fleet—and that means room for another full-time apprentice pilot. Are you interested?"

"A *what?*"

"Second to me, of course—"

The coffee flew across the room as Mike jumped out of his seat, shouting, "*Pilot? Do you mean it? Pilot?*"

Twyla glanced at Lek. "Do you think that means 'yes'?"

"I think so," Lek said.

Mike was grinning at them from ear to ear, a great shout welling up inside him. He stamped his feet gleefully.

"He's lost it," Lek said.

"The boy's crazy . . ."

Mike threw his hands up with abandon. "*Eee-yowwwweee! . . .*"

TECHNICAL DATA

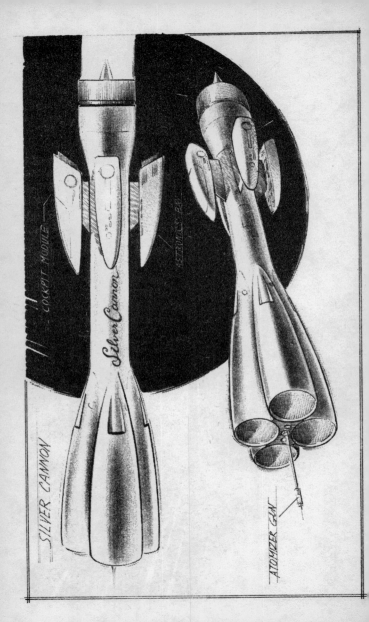

COCKPIT MODULE

ASTRALLIAN RAY

SILVER CANNON

Silver Cannon

ATOMIZER GUN

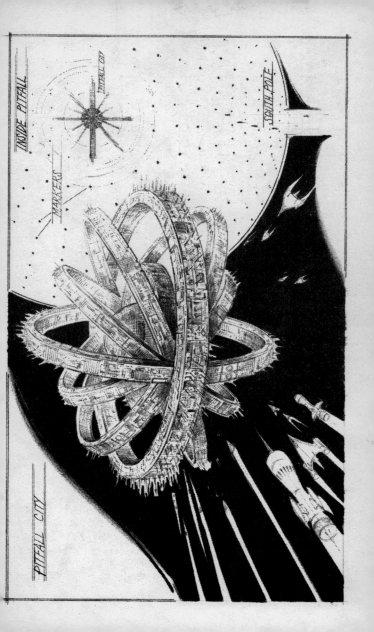

INSIDE PITFALL

SOUTH POLE

MARKERS

PITFALL CITY

PITFALL CITY

PITFALL CITY

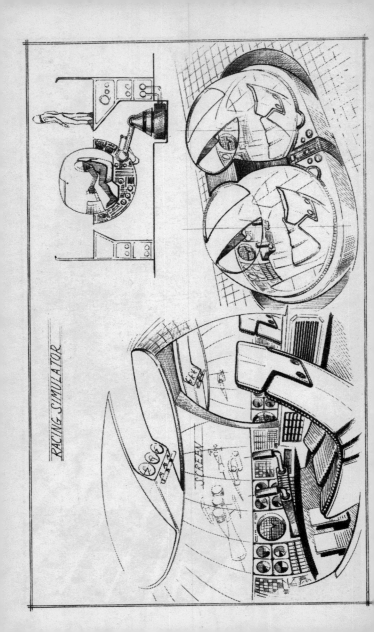

RACING SIMULATOR

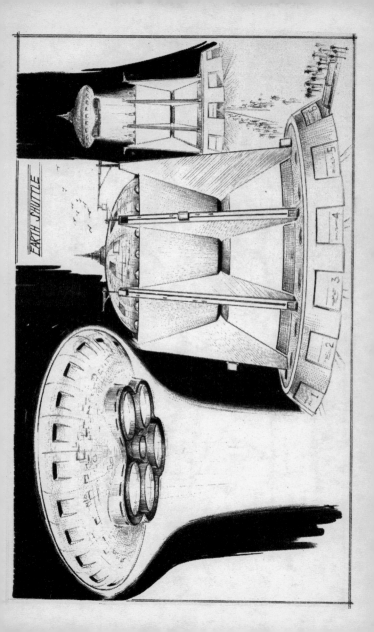

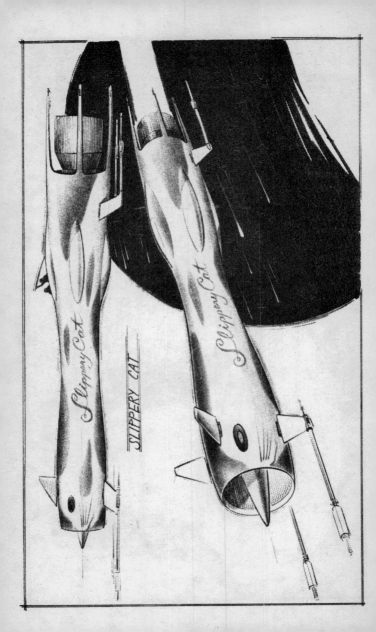

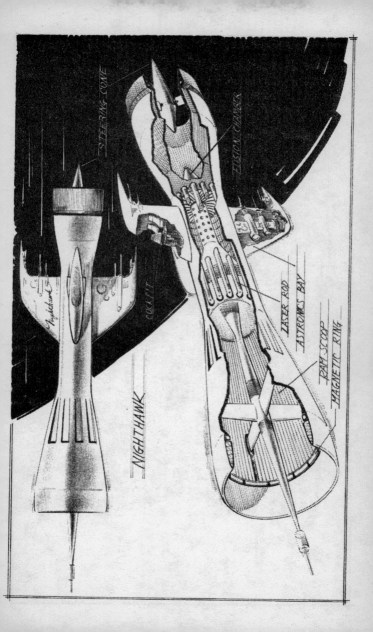

STEERING CONE

FISSION CHAMBER

Nighthawk

COCKPIT

LASER ROD

ASTRONICS BAY

RAM SCOOP

MAGNETIC RING

NIGHTHAWK

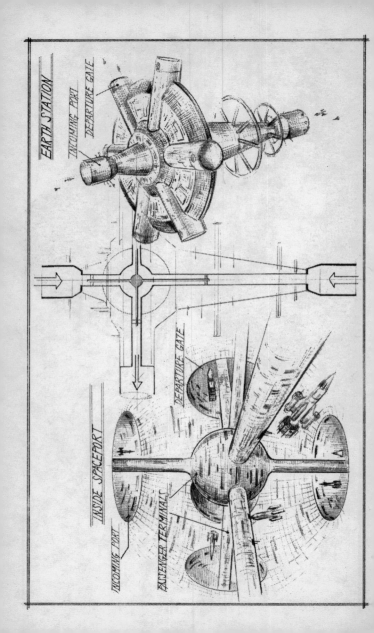

EARTH STATION

INCOMING PORT

DEPARTURE GATE

INSIDE SPACEPORT

DEPARTURE GATE

INCOMING PORT

PASSENGER TERMINAL

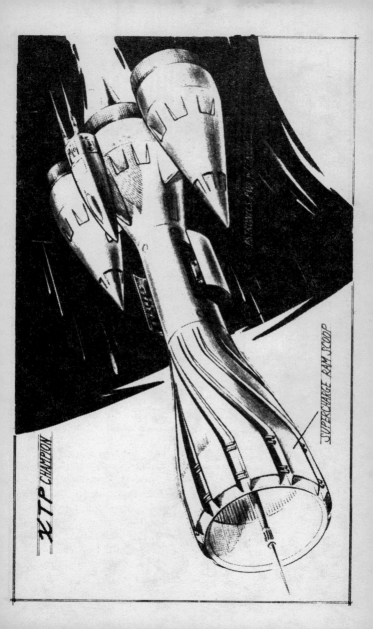

XTP CHAMPION

SUPERCHARGE RAM SCOOP

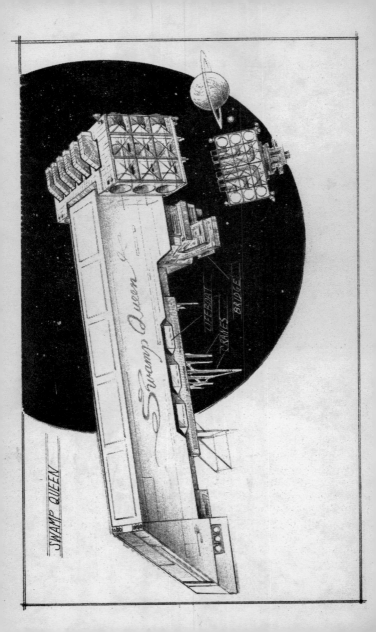

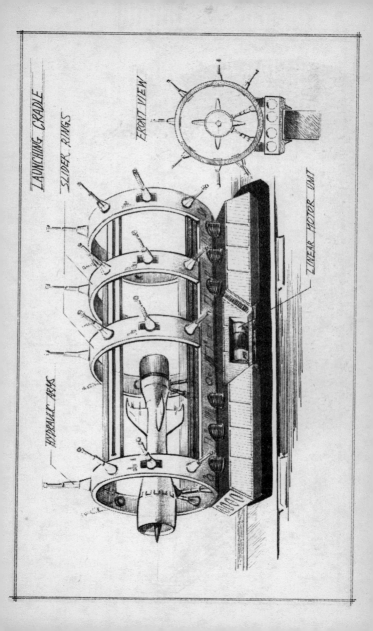

LAUNCHING CRADLE

SLIDER RINGS

FRONT VIEW

HYDRAULIC ARMS

LINEAR MOTOR UNIT

RACING COURSE MAP

RACING COURSES, CLYPSIS,
PITFALL & ENIGMA

CLYPSIS
PITFALL

ENIGMA

COMING IN JANUARY . . .
VOLUME TWO IN

ROGER ZELAZNY'S
ALIEN SPEEDWAY

PITFALL

By Thomas Wylde